to sway a Vagabond

tempting thieves

STEPHANIE BWABWA

To Sway A Vagabond is a work of fiction. Names, characters, places, and incidents are the product of the author's imagination or have been used to create this work of art.

Any similarities to actual persons, living or dead, events, etc. is completely coincidental.

Published by: Elledelle Entertainment

To Sway A Vagabond. 1st ed.

Cover Digital Design: Saint Jupiter

Cover Illustration: Ireen Chau

Formatting by: Elledelle Entertainment

Vagabonds deserve love and a second chance, too. If that's you, may you find a kindred spirit with these angels.

READER NOTE

Dear Elledellien,

For your convenience, you'll find a glossary towards the back of this book to help you with pronunciations, definitions, and translations.

Enjoy the tale.

Wings high! Welcome to Elledelle.

— Stephanie

CHAPTER 1

FABIENNE

Everyone knew kings were meant to be robbed. Especially from their graves. But this dusknite, Fabienne Evruel found robbing a king, while he still breathed, a much better proposition. Tonight, she was here for her ticket to freedom, and she wasn't going to leave without it.

Fabienne blinked in the darkness, breathing in the cool, crisp air. It filled her lungs, her veins, and enlivened her wings. A gentle breeze passed through the bedchamber where she hovered, her wings pulsing lightly, as she keenly watched the Armands snore away below. They slept like the dead, their chests rising and falling, completely unaware of her presence in the shadows.

With precision, Fabienne noted the subtle pulse of their wings, as if the wings themselves were alive and in the middle of being refreshed. All six of their membranous pairs were intertwined, layered one atop the other, as their bodies—plump like fattened Shadowboars after too many meals—rolled over between the plush coverlets.

The Armands were the tyrannical, and pompous, King and Queen of the Xodom Megalopolis. They held immense power throughout the dark and corrupt city, lording over the angelic citizenry with tight fists.

Fabienne watched them sleep, cataloguing every breath and movement. Every dreamy whisper. Every untoward secret they'd be horrified to learn someone else knew. She had planned extensively for this moment, spending the better part of twelve dawns in preparation. Every day she'd flown to the palace, searching for her mark, and plotting how to get it with one seamless break-in.

The Armand Palàs—a gargantuan structure of high walls and fortified entries—was a mighty fortress lined with gilded halls and gemstone barriers.

The Armand royals were affluent, descending from angels who'd held the throne of Xodom's Southern Sector in their grip from the Ninth Age until the present—the Thirteenth Age. They also had a knack for hoarding artifacts and heirlooms of great value.

This dusknite, Fabienne planned to help herself to one of those heirlooms. If she was successful, from now on, her entire life was going to change.

Wind whispered through the high arched corridors, brushing against the stone columns etched with Domènn script. For a moment, Fabienne paused, reading the words inscribed in the native language of Domenents, her angelic rank of origin.

Kun nous vini, nous wè. Kun nous wè, nous konkeri. Kun nous konkeri, nous dirije. Kukaan ei kenbe tèt non résiste.

Fabienne's nostrils flared.

When we come, we see. When we see, we conquer. When we conquer, we rule. None can withstand us.

Fabienne gathered her nerve. Fear of powerful angelic fanmèris, and their long-standing legacies, had since been broken out of her. Trespassing into the Armand Palàs was bold and dangerous, but it wouldn't deter her. She had a job to do.

She continued floating just below the vaulted ceiling, wings spread wide, her movements silent as the shadows. Muted lights flickered below. Six pairs of obsidian, membranous wings framed her silhouette, nearly identical to that of the Armand King and his Soulu. The faintest glint of her ethèr—her innate angelic power—casted a soft glow against the wing's edges. She needed to be careful how she used the power. Ethèr was not only visible when drawn, it was also traceable.

Fabienne's eyes locked onto the pretty glass case with her mark inside. She sucked in a sharp, silent breath as her hearts, all six, pounded wildly in her chest with growing adrenaline. She couldn't look away from the target, her mouth salivating at the thought of how it felt to the touch.

Fabienne stared down at the enchanting, silver locket looped through an iridescent ring, the ivory stone at its center pulsing faintly, alive. *Zazràs* was what everyone called it.

It was both a locket and a cage.

Inside the stone was shackled the fôrs of a Fallen. How had the spirit of a fallen angel been siphoned from its body, then fused into the stone, trapping the Fallen angel for an endless eternity? She'd never guess. The Fallen was still alive, just with no physical body to return to, chained to this piece of rock. It was a miserable way to exist.

Fabienne almost felt sorry for the Fallen.

Almost.

Zazràs had remained in Armand possession for over a millennia. This dusknite, that would change.

Fabienne took a steadying breath and let herself drop. Air rushed past her, the controlled descent precise. She landed without a sound, her booted feet meeting the luxurious carpet as she straightened, wings folding neatly behind her. Her movements were calculated, every step deliberate. She couldn't, *wouldn't*, afford a single mistake.

A quick sweep of the bedchamber confirmed what she'd planned for. She was completely alone. The Palàs Watcher—the hired guardian of the Armand fanmèri, and trained to kill on sight—was somewhere in the hall with drool dribbling down her chin as she slept like an idiot.

If everything went like expected, Fabienne would be long gone before the rotpot stirred from the elixir Fabienne had slipped into her meal earlier.

Fabienne wore darkness like a second skin, clad in a muted, silver tunic beneath an onyx, battle-kaftan to the knees over matching angel-tights for ease of movement. Twin daggers, made with shadowglass, lay tucked against the curve of her waist, hidden beneath the dark folds. Her fingers brushed against their hilts out of habit.

The chamber was vast with heirlooms, of all shapes, sizes, and economical value, encased in glass pedestals lining the oval perimeter. At the center of it all, atop a marble dais, rested *Zazràs*. The ivory stone pulsed, almost as if the Fallen inside could sense her presence.

Fabienne drew a slow, measured breath. She lifted

both of her palms, opened the eyes of her fôrs, and began drawing on her ethèr. Her spirit came alive as her powers began surging through her body, warming her blood. Ethèr coursed through her veins until the flow reached her palms. She concentrated on it now, making sure to keep the golden, shadowy substance muted, as not to wake the Armands. She flexed her palms, releasing her ethèr. The chamber trembled faintly in response. Fabienne froze.

She didn't dare move. Breathe. After a long pause, she loosed a small, heavy breath. Sweat beat at her temples. She got annoyed, almost calling herself a rotpot out loud.

Burning stars.

This was supposed to be an easy job and already she was making foolish mistakes.

Focus.

No one stirred. The draw of her ethèr wasn't enough to wake the Palàs Watcher, but it was enough for her to feel the pulse of life threading through the air. Domenent-angel ethèr was enhancement-based. In her case, as a Void Reaver, her distinct affinity allowed her to amplify precision. She was an expert in locating a weakness in any angel, or thing, and exposing it. She focused on that now—heightening her senses, sharpening her awareness. She poked and prodded, searching for the weak points of the glass case so it could be broken. Then she would take the heirloom.

A rustle of wings caught her attention. Fabienne stilled, listening. When she last checked, the Watcher had been stationed beyond the archway, dozing. Fabienne twitched the winged curves of her ears, stretching her capacity to hear more, farther. That's when she caught the light rustle of wings and boots dragging against carpet. The Palàs Watcher was just outside of the bedchamber, pacing.

Rot.

Fabienne fought the urge to suck her teeth out of irritation. The Watcher should still be asleep. The tincture should've kept her unconscious for several hôrs yet. It hadn't even been a full hour and already she'd woken up. But how?

Fabienne frowned, quickly thinking of what she'd have to do if faced with a confrontation. She had mapped the Watchers rotations for six dawns, learning the rhythm of the Watcher's steps, and flight trails, as intimately as she knew the breath in her lungs.

Fabienne listened close, tracking the Watchers movements now. She allowed her breathing to slow, calming her nerves. The Watcher wouldn't enter the bedchamber unless disturbed. Fabienne still had time. She just needed to be extremely quiet. And fast.

With a flick of her wrist, she produced a thin glass shard, its edges laced with ethèr. Pressing it against the pedestals locking mechanism, she channeled a controlled current through it, unraveling the locks woven through the glass with practiced ease.

A soft *click* sounded.

The seal broke.

Fabienne watched the protective shield shimmer before vanishing. She reached forward, her fingers grazing the cold silver of the locket. The moment her skin made contact, a pulse of something ancient, something wicked, rippled through her fôrs.

The chamber seemed to breathe.

A warning.

Fabienne retracted her hand with controlled quiet, moving to pocket the stone in her satchel, when movement surfaced beyond the bedchambers archway. Fabienne's blood ran cold.

"Drop it, Reaver," snarled the Palàs Watcher.

CHAPTER 2
FABIENNE

Fabienne met the eyes of the Palàs Watcher. She was a vision of harsh beauty and vengeance personified, cloaked in obsidian and emerald livery. In the Watcher's multicolored eyes of honey and earth, a brewing storm swirled. That glare promised brutal punishment for Fabienne when she was caught.

Fabienne swallowed around a tight knot in her throat. For a moment, everything froze as the two stared one another down. Then, quick as a flash, Fabienne slammed all six pairs of her wings together. The clap was deafening, stunning the angel with temporary shock. Fabienne spun around herself, secured *Zazràs* in her satchel, then bolted.

"Watchers, wings high! The Reaver has come!"

The Watcher's voice thundered with a current of

hatred so strong Fabienne felt it echo through her bones. Like a clarion call, it reverberated against the palàs walls.

Chandeliers flared to life on their own, flooding the bedchamber with light. The hum of ethèr crackled in the air, angelic power swelling and suffocating. The pounding of beating wings sent a fresh surge of urgency through Fabienne's veins.

Burning stars.

This wasn't how any of this was supposed to go.

Fabienne unfurled her wings in a single, powerful beat, launching herself upward just as armored Watchers flooded into the bedchamber. A bolt of onyx ethèr whistled past her ear, missing by mere inches. Fabienne twisted midair, soaring toward the upper ledges, her satchel cooling with the pulsing stone, as she propelled herself forward.

The Watchers shouted, their wings spreading as they took flight to give chase, but she had the advantage. Fabienne had memorized every necessary inch of this palàs. They could chase her down all they wanted, but she would get out. She would finish this job and she would be free.

Somewhere below, amidst the fray, the Armands stirred.

"The locket is gone! She took *Zazràs*! Get it back you useless pieces of ashen rot. *Now*."

Fabienne could have laughed. The screaming came from Ayella Armand. The Lady of this palàs—an overweight asheater—couldn't lift a finger to protect what was valuable to her, even if all of her angelic life-cycles depended on it.

Ignoring them all, Fabienne locked in, focused on getting out. Dipping low, Fabienne began weaving between golden archways and sweeping columns. The vast hall blurred around her, speed turning the world into streaks of light and shadow. The cool air roared in her ears, the pulse of her ethèr fueling every passing second.

"I will drench you in shale-acid, and set you on fire until your fôrs dissipates into the ashes you belong in," the leading Palàs Watcher seethed. "You will not survive this, Reaver. Having your wings plucked and snapped, like your brittle neck, will be a mercy."

Fabienne snorted. "All that talking," she mumbled, spinning over herself in the air. "And for what?"

She raced across the palàs heading for freedom. She had the locket and that's all that mattered. With it in her possession, everything would change. Her life depended on it.

So did Tatiana's, her sisari.

The thought of her little sister was like a stab between her ribs. The pain was sharp and poignant.

Exactly what she needed to concentrate and get out of this stars-forsaken palàs.

The escape route was ahead. A hidden passage behind the grand biblion. If she could just reach the library before they closed in—

A bolt of ethèr shot past her.

Fabienne barely managed to twist her body, avoiding the searing energy by a hair's breadth. The heat singed the edge of her sleeve. Fabienne pressed harder across the palace, forcing her wings faster. Her hearts raced as she fought for escape from the Watchers who were still charging in pursuit.

She clenched her jaw and pushed harder, diving into a steep drop before catching the updraft, using the momentum to slingshot herself forward. The biblion's towering entrance loomed ahead, its gilded doors parted just enough to slip through. At the back of the library, her escape route awaited her.

She leaned forward in her flight, racing for the opening.

Then a brutal force slammed into her from behind.

Pain exploded across her back, a searing jolt that locked her wings for half a breath. She tumbled, vision spinning, and scarcely managed to right herself before she crashed into the floor. Her satchel slipped off, rolling across the carpet towards a curtain.

Fabienne winced, laggardly forcing herself upright.

Move Fabienne, move! She chided herself.

She lunged for the satchel with one of her wings, and spun around in one fluid motion to strap it back on, while preparing to defend herself. The Palàs Watchers descended like Bloodwood Hyenas, their wings spread and weapons drawn. She counted four. No, five. Six?

Too many.

"Xodom dung. It's time we were rid of your existence, once and for all."

Rot.

Fabienne's fingers brushed the hilts of her daggers. She let a swell of ethèr warm her blood. Quickly she ran through her options. She could fight. She could make them bleed. Sift out their weak points and unravel their minds from within before obliterating them. But that would mean delaying her escape and wasting precious time she didn't have.

Tatiana's face flashed in her mind again.

Fighting her way out wasn't an option.

Not this dusknite.

Fabienne exhaled sharply, steeling herself. Then, without hesitation, she flung herself toward the nearest Watcher. He reacted on instinct, swiping at her chest with a pair of his wings. She twisted mid-flight, evading the strike with effortless grace, and used the momentum to propel herself upward. Her wings snapped open, catching the air, and she vaulted over them in a fluid arc. Bending backwards, careening past the slew of Palàs Watchers, Fabienne shot down to land on the other side.

The moment her feet touched the floor, she *ran.* Flying would do her no good where she was trying to enter. The biblion was no longer an option. Fabienne pivoted for her next choice—the hidden passage by the obscure fireplace in the East Wing. It wasn't too far from where she was. She ran with all her might, cutting around a hall racing across the lush carpet floors.

The hidden panel grew within reach.

Fabienne shot for the small door, bending low. She pressed her palm against the etched sigils, pouring ethèr into the ancient lock. Her stomach twisted.

Nothing happened.

The mechanism had been jammed.

"You can't be serious," she seethed. "I swear this is Ehyeh repaying me for my sins." She snarled, slamming her hand against the grate. “Of all the times you could make me an example, you choose now?”

A heavy presence loomed behind her.

Palàs Watchers.

Fabienne pivoted just in time to see one raise her wings like weapons, their membranous edges sharpened like blades, the talons curling like hooks. Her wings gleamed under the blinding lights of the hall.

The Palàs Watcher struck.

Fabienne dodged—narrowly. The talon of the Watcher's wing nicked her sleeve, cutting through the fabric, grazing her skin. Scorching heat licked her arm, but she didn't falter. There wasn't any time.

"Ehyeh, come on. *Please.* Help. I need your help!"

Fabienne tried the small door one more time. No luck. It didn't budge.

"Now what in the hèls is the actual point of praying..." She trailed off, vexed.

Fabienne blinked over her shoulders at the Watchers closing in from behind. She huffed. Then made a decision. Forget the hidden passage. She'd ran out of time. She had to get out of the palàs *now.*

Fabienne pivoted sharply, shooting to her feet from her crouch, throwing herself into a ram-rod dive, like a spear with perfect aim. The Watchers lunged for her, but she was already moving, already slipping past their reach. She unfurled her wings in a violent snap, thrusting herself through the nearest stained-glass window. The explosion of glass and ethèr shattered the dusk.

Lights began flickering on across the length of the palàs.

Wind howled as she shot into the open air, shards of colored light cascading around her. The city sprawled ahead, an endless labyrinth of towering spires and twisting alleys.

Behind her, the palàs raged. And Fabienne grinned.

Drips of golden blood trickled down her mahogany-hued arms where the glass shards had sliced through the sleeves of her tunic. Some of her knuckles had also tasted the bite of their sting.

But she had *Zazràs*.

All six wing pairs spread wide, Fabienne shot into the dusknite, weaving through alleys and towers with supernatural speed. She chuckled to herself, proud of the feat. The dusk should've gone smoother, but now none of that mattered.

She'd finished the job. Gotten the locket.

Which meant, she could now pay her blood debt, and finally be free.

CHAPTER 3

EMMANUEL

Every angel with ethèr in their fôrs knew kings were meant to be robbed. Especially from their graves. But robbing a thief? That game was infinitely more dangerous, and just downright fun, to play.

Emmanuel Alfonse hovered high above Xodom, his six pairs of membranous wings spread wide, gliding through the megalopolis's thick air. His wings, dark as midnight with iridescent veins of molten gold, caught the nightlime's fractured glow as he rode the shifting currents. Xodom sprawled beneath him—a labyrinth of towering spires, crumbling bridges, and twisting alleyways drowning in shadows and aged blood. Ethèr-lit lanterns flickered like fireflies below, some steady, others sputtering from the grit and filth that coated the megalopolis.

Even from this height, Emmanuel could taste the city—stone dust, the bitter tang of oil-fueled torches, the acrid bite of the Onyx River, slithering like a diseased serpent through its belly, with a putrid stench of rot to boot.

Xodom was alive in the deadliest way.

Like all of its angelic citizenry, it had more than one heartbeat. Which turned out more often to be a curse.

Xodom was home to a dark, restless rhythm of crime and power, of rulers and rebels, of angels who had long since abandoned their eternal charge. The streets pulsed with secrets whispered in the tongues of merchants selling fraudulent wares, and empty bargains, beneath flickering torchlight.

Lovers met in shadowed corridors, breaking oaths to the mates they'd bonded to in an Age past. Beggars and thieves navigated the veins of the city like flies coursing through a decaying corpse.

Xodom was the city that never slept.

Now it pulsed beneath Emmanuel, its towers clawing toward the forsaken heavens, as if it could reach beyond its own depravity. The hum of energy, the low vibration of millions of lives interwoven into the fabric of the city, was almost hypnotic.

Emmanuel loved Xodom almost as much as he hated it.

And at its pulsing core, the Armand Palàs blazed like a beacon against the gloom, golden halls scintillating beneath its illumination. It stood tall and proud, a mockery to the rising poverty among the city's struggling Domenents. He let his gaze track downward, to the shattered remnants of a stained-glass window that glittered across the rooftops like fallen stars.

A clean escape.

A dark, vicious grin curled his lips as he adjusted his grip on the silver locket dangling from his fingers. The air around it vibrated with an unseen force, making his skin itch with residual energy.

"Wings high, Reaver," he purred, even though she flew far into the dusk away from him. "So close to a job well done... yet still so far."

Emmanuel *tsked*, his voice a whisper. Then he chuckled, the low rumble filling his chest, as his gaze traced the rushing flight of the thief.

Reaver.

Emmanuel almost shivered at the thought of her name. Throughout Xodom's darkest alleys it brought fear. Terror. She was a Void Reaver, a Domenent angel able to sift out weaknesses and utterly ruin whoever had the gall to get in her way.

Domenents who were Void Reavers weren't common. Their abilities were rare, making them even more terrifying. And she was the most powerful one, ever lurking in Xodom's shadows, finishing job after job for her bosses.

Emmanuel grinned wide with pride.

Calculated as Reaver was, he'd still been able to pawn the locket in the middle of her heist while she fought off the Palàs Watchers. Messing with her plans by waking them up, had all been too easy. A shame. She was so precise. Methodical.

Boring.

He had been watching her for dawns now, curious. She'd stalked the Armand Palàs each dawn, often making notes in some unseen scroll. She was skilled, meticulous—way too careful for a thief.

Emmanuel preferred a little chaos. A little spontaneity. It made things more interesting. More fun. Now, because of that difference between them, he held the very stone she'd risked everything to get her hands on. He sucked his teeth, shaking his head. All her efforts had been a waste.

The wind shifted, carrying with it the distant clang of metal on stone, the rustling of wings in the dusknite. Below him, a squadron of winged guards sliced through the air, their emerald and obsidian armor gleaming under the half-light. Their wings—stiff, disciplined—flared in perfect formation as they scanned the streets below. Looking for her.

Emmanuel squinted to get a better look.

It was the Palàs Watchers.

He yawned. They were such bores. Full of order, structure, and a need to obey the creed. As if Xodomite angels actually took the law serious.

Stretching until his bones popped, Emmanuel sighed contentedly, tilting his wings and descending into a slow spiral. He wasn't worried about getting caught with the locket. He had played this game too long to be found. Now what he needed was some spiced angel-wine and a pretty thing dressed in just her hair to go with it.

Emmanuel landed silently atop a domed cathedral, the cracked mosaic tiles shifting under his boots. Xodom stretched before him in all its sprawling, corrupted glory. The city pulsed with life and he was ready to join it. A certain tavern was calling his name. He flipped the silver locket between his fingers, watching the ivory stone at its center pulse faintly. Warm. *Alive.*

His ethèr twitched in response.

This thing was dangerous.

He had stolen plenty of heirlooms before, but nothing quite like this. He didn't know much about why the Armands had hoarded *Zazràs*, but he knew it wasn't just an heirloom—it was power. And power always came with a price.

His multicolored eyes—amber and honey—narrowed slightly. *Why was she after this?*

A disturbance rippled through the air, arresting his attention. There was an uncomfortable bend in the night. Though it was subtle, it was enough to put him on edge. He pocketed the locket and turned. A presence was watching him.

Emmanuel didn't startle easily, but something in the pit of his stomach screamed out in alarm. He rolled his shoulders, feigning nonchalance, as he scanned the rooftops. Nothing but the city's shadows stretched around him. Then, there was a whisper of movement. And another tear in the air.

Emmanuel flexed his hands, letting his ethèr unfurl just slightly, amplifying his senses. The dusk deepened. The shadows thickened.

Then he saw them.

Perched across the way, just beyond the edge of another tower, stood a figure wreathed in darkness. This was no common Domenent. Not a Watcher. Not even a Sherèf—although officers were usually out patrolling at this time.

He shuddered.

It was a Shaith.

Emmanuel's blood went cold.

The wraith-like creature was still, its lanky frame wrapped in a haze of shadow and oblivion. Its deformed wings barely twitched, a mockery of what they once were. Its eyes—dark, endless, swimming with unnatural life—locked onto him with predatory intent.

Rot.

Emmanuel let out a slow breath. Shaiths weren't just monsters, brutal killers; they were also trackers, serving masters for a high price. And their payment was never in coin.

Emmanuel felt a rising sickness blossom in his chest. If he was being tracked by Shaiths, he was in a rotting realm of trouble.

The Shaith tilted its head. Its voice slithered across the dusknite.

"You're a fool for crossing the Fraetèn."

CHAPTER 4

EMMANUEL

The growing darkness in the sky mocked Emmanuel's pride. A chill crawled up his spine. He didn't react. He wouldn't give that *thing* the satisfaction. Instead, he let his smirk return, masking the unease rolling beneath his skin.

"Am I?" he mused, voice easy. Almost like he was telling an enraptured audience a really good joke. He laughed. "Funny. I don't remember having any encounters with the Fraetèn." A pause. "On purpose."

The Shaith didn't blink. "What you stole from the aèl belongs to them."

Of course this was about *Zazràs*.

Emmanuel sighed dramatically, running a hand through his short, copper-red locs. Something twinged in his chest at the Shaith referring to Reaver as no more than a youngling girl. *The aèl.* For some reason he didn't like the sound of it. Especially from the tongue of the walking dead.

"Look, I *borrow* things all the time. It's a service, really. You'd be surprised how much I return... for a price."

The creature's voice slithered through the air. "Don't play coy with me, Vagabond."

Emmanuel stiffened.

That title.

He hated the sound of it coming from the Shaith's mouth. It ground his nerves, setting him on edge. Emmanuel drew on his ethèr, his powers swelling with his anger, his cool mask slipping.

"As far as I'm concerned, you and the Fraetèn can piss off. I don't have anything to do with the Noir-mother and her syndicate."

The shadows around the Shaith deepened. "You will."

A flicker of movement in the distance caught Emmanuel's eye. Shadows stirred across the heights of the megalopolis, prowling, silent, and methodical. There were more of them.

Emmanuel wouldn't entertain the creature any longer. In a single, fluid motion, he unfurled his wings and launched himself into the sky. He flew low, wings slicing through the currents above Xodom's underbelly.

The weight of *Zazràs* pulsed in the pocket at his thigh where he'd secured it. The locket's unnatural warmth pressed into his thigh like a heartbeat. His mind raced. He had stolen plenty of things in his time—gilded artifacts, cursed heirlooms, entire fortunes ripped from the hands of fools who thought power made them untouchable.

But this? This was different.

He could feel it in the way the city breathed around him.

What you stole from the aèl belongs to them.

Emmanuel wondered what exactly *Zazràs* was. There was no way all of this fuss was happening for some ordinary locket. Especially not if the Fraeten—one of Xodom's most powerful, and most dangerous, crime syndicates—were involved.

Again he wondered what Reaver wanted with it.

He veered sharply, cutting past the crumbling terraces of the city's southern quarter, his boots skimming the edge of a sagging balcony before he landed lightly against the rooftop. The thick, obsidian stones beneath him were warm, and hard. He crouched low, fingers brushing against the jagged stone as he surveyed the alleys around him.

Still. It was all too still.

He was being followed. But it wasn't only Shaiths on his tail. He squinted at the darkness, then a slow grin curled his full lips. *She* was following him, too.

Emmanuel chuckled darkly. It took her long enough to find out her satchel was a little light. Reaver had come to reclaim the locket. He snorted, genuinely amused. He had no plans to hand it over. He took in a deep, steadying breath. He needed to move. Shake them all off. And fast.

The streets writhed with Xodom's darkness. Somewhere in this chaos, Emmanuel had a contact, and needed to reach them before the Shaiths, and Reaver, reached him.

Emmanuel flew soundlessly to a ledge, moving with the ease of someone who belonged everywhere and nowhere at once. He led a dance through the skies, before dipping into the streets. The Shaiths didn't take the bait.

Reaver did.

She trailed him, keeping close to his heels. More than once, he slowed enough for her hand to brush close, the tips of their fingers grazing one another's, then he shot away, peeling off into the dark of the dusknite. He could hear her curse from behind him. He laughed and kept flying, weaving, and dodging her, until he shook her off completely.

He slipped into the shadows of a certain side

street, moving quickly, weaving through the thick press of Domenent bodies and wings that filled the shadow-market. Lantern light flickered off membranous wings and sharpened blades. The scent of roasted meat clashed with the underlying stench of sweat and rusting metal. Emmanuel moved with stealth, his steps sure, weaving through the cracks of Xodom's heartbeats, leading him toward the one place he'd get answers.

The entrance to the Crying Veil was tucked into the ruins of an old temple, hidden beneath layers of enchanted ethèr. To most angels, it was nothing but a collapsed hall of shattered columns and forgotten prayers.

To him?

It was a portal entry.

He pressed his palm against the crumbling stone, feeling for the familiar flow of ethèr. The power hummed beneath his skin, pulsed once—then let him through. The world flickered. And then he was inside.

The Crying Veil wasn't like the rest of Xodom. It was older. Darker. A place where information was currency, and death was just another trade. The air was thick with the scent of old parchment and spiced incense, laced with the distant hum of whispered deals. Shrouded figures moved between the lantern-lit stalls, their voices low and clipped.

A zobàtant—an angelic pit fighter—bartered over an obsidian blade, his wings twitching as he spoke in rushed tones. A Crescent—an angelic assassin—stood at the far end, watching. Waiting.

Emmanuel was wary of the Crescent. They were Transcendents, angels of Higherank then Domenents, with ethèr they used to lord over Loweranks. They were incomprehensibly beautiful, intelligent, powerful, and horrifyingly brutal. Crescents never erred on the side of mercy, and they liked to make their marks suffer. Wherever Crescents were, he didn't want to be. He had to make this visit quick.

Avoiding eye contact with the Crescent, Emmanuel floated to the end of the Crying Veil. Beneath the glow of an ancient chandelier, an angel —gorgeous and wicked as a grave—watched him from her usual perch, sipping from an obsidian cup. Emmanuel didn't hesitate. He moved toward her with purpose, sliding into the empty seat across from her before she could object.

"Tell me you didn't do something stupid," she said, coolly.

He flashed her a grin. "Yolanda. Now you know you'll have to be more specific than that. How exactly are you defining stupid?"

Yolanda sighed. "Always finding new ways to get on my nerves, eh, Havoc?"

Her voice was smooth, but her eyes were sharp, calculating. Emmanuel looked at Yolanda, wondering what was going through her mind. Something in her tone hinted at trouble. If she was looking at him like this, it meant his name was moving through the streets.

He leaned back. "Spit it out, Yola. My head. What's the price now?"

Yolanda blinked back, tilting her head. "With you dead or alive?"

"Darling, you know I always prefer alive." He grinned.

"Pity." She bat her pretty lashes, meeting his gaze, her beautifully exposed brown skin glowing in the low light. "The Fraetèn are offering quite a bit to see you Clipped. Siphoned, even."

Emmanuel exhaled through his nose. "Where do the Shaiths come in?"

Yolanda's expression darkened.

That wasn't a good sign.

"My Havoc. You already know this," she mused. "The Shaiths don't care for coin. They feed on fôrs. It just so happens they prefer to feast on the spirits of angels who like to run. Shaiths always love a good hunt."

She flashed her teeth at him knowingly. Something cold curled in Emmanuel's gut.

Yolanda blinked at Emmanuel's waist, then her gaze lowered to the bulge between his legs, lingering long enough to make him blush deep. Without shame, she let her gaze lazily slide down the length of his thigh, before they came to rest on his pocket. She nodded at the buckle.

"What did you steal, Havoc?"

He hesitated.

Yolanda waited.

He swallowed, voice low. "*Zazràs*. Pilfered it off of Reaver after she snagged it from the Armands."

Yolanda was expressionless, but the blaze in her multicolored, lavender and indigo eyes, told him all he needed to know about the locket.

"Get rid of it."

"No." His fingers tightened around the edge of the table.

"Emmanuel," she hissed.

He flinched at the unfamiliar sound of his real name being spoken aloud. In the Crying Veil, no less. Few angels knew him by name, and he planned to keep it that way. His nostrils flared. His ethèr swam, demanding retribution. He'd ended the lives of offending angels for less. Had she lost her rotting mind?

"I'm not kidding," she continued, oblivious to the

tension in his neck. His curling fists. Fear crept into her voice. "You don't know what you're toying with. You have no clue how many will stop at nothing to get it. Even if they have to carve it out of your cold, dead, carcass. Emmanuel. You're reckless, but not a fool. Please," she pleaded. "Get rid of it. This dusknite."

The weight of her words settled into his ribs. His throat tightened.

"Tell me something, Yolanda," he said, his voice mere breath over the small table. The Crying Veil suddenly felt suffocating. Too many bodies, too many eyes, too many enemies. "What *is Zazràs*? What did I steal from the Void Reaver?"

Yolanda's expression radiated fear he'd never seen before. She exhaled through her nose, leaning in close, dropping her voice so only he could hear.

"*Zazràs* isn't a stone. It's not a locket, either. It's a cage." Her eyes flashed. "With the fôrs of a Fallen angel trapped inside. Pretty sure it's a Shetani."

What in all the burning hèls?

A Fallen who was once an Etherien angel from the Syëlle rank? Syëlles were even higher in rank than Transcendents.

Rot.

Yolanda continued, clearly oblivious to Emmanuel's inner turmoil. "And the Fallen still *lives.*

You didn’t steal an ancient heirloom, Havoc." Her eyes burned. "You stole a death sentence."

CHAPTER 5
FABIENNE

The megalopolis of Xodom stretched wide beneath Fabienne as she soared above its maze of towering spires and golden bridges. Wind sliced through her thigh-length locs, her six pairs of wings working in fluid synchronization to keep her aloft. The crisp, dusky air did little to cool the heat simmering in her blood.

Zazràs was gone.

Her hands clenched as she pushed higher, her breathing tight with frustration. She had done everything right. She'd studied the Armand Palàs for dawns, mapped its security patterns, accounted for every possible complication—except for another meddling thief getting in her way.

She had been tearing through Xodom's alleys, racing away from the Armand Palàs Watchers when a scent, strong, heady, and slightly familiar, had hit her. An alarm had gone off in her mind. Then she'd felt her satchel. Sure enough. The locket had been stolen.

Fabienne's jaw tightened as a thought flashed across her mind. There had been another angelic shadow in the palàs. She replayed the job over and over in her mind. The Watcher's alarm. Flashes of movement from all sides. The figure perched in the shadows close to the curtains, watching. Calculating.

Whoever he was, he'd intentionally planned to foil the job. And it rotting worked. She'd been too focused on securing *Zazràs* to even notice. Now she was paying for it.

Fabienne frowned, a frustrated growl building in the back of her throat. She tilted her wings, banking into a sharp dive that carried her over the rooftops. The eerie glow of Xodom's low-lit streets blurred beneath her, casting long shadows against the grime-slicked domes and broken bridges.

The Southern Sector pulsed with ethèr, majik, and dark memories, alive in the worst ways. If the thief had any sense, he would be disappearing into the underbelly of the city by now. But she had a feeling he wasn't the type to hide. Not before coming out to play first.

She knew angels like him well. It was the nature of the life she lived. They were reckless. Arrogant. The kind who played with fire just to see how close they could get before being burned. No. He wasn't hiding. He was watching. Waiting. And she would find him.

Fabienne landed in the quieter stretch of Xodom's inner district, her boots hitting the cobblestone with practiced silence. The scent of embers and spice filled the air, carried from the open fires of late-night vendors. Rusted chimes clinked with the breeze. Voices murmured in shadowed alleys, and exchanges were made in hush tones. This was the part of the city where secrets thrived.

Fabienne moved through it like a ghost.

She reached for her ethèr, sharpening her senses, stretching her awareness into the space around her. The ripple of energy flickered across her skin like a phantom touch, revealing the rhythm of life beyond what the eye could see. She found movement in the east alley. When she sharpened her senses further, she found a figure perched three stories above. That had to be him.

Fabienne adjusted her grip on the dagger tucked beneath the folds of her fitted skirt and ascended. Her wings unfurled, dark as the midnight sky, propelling her upward with five strong beats. She landed lightly on the edge of a rooftop, her gaze locked onto the distant glow of shuffling figures. She floated over stealthily, closing in. The scent of burnt ozone hit her first.

Then came the unnatural stillness.

Fabienne froze mid-flight, her wings tucking close as she took in the scene. The rooftop across from hers was empty—but not unoccupied. The shadows curled unnaturally, bending around an unseen presence. The air trembled with majik, thick and suffocating. It was the kind of energy that belonged to one being alone. But as wicked as Xodom was, there were no Fallen angels roaming about loose. Which left only one other option as to what the figure was.

A Shaith.

Fabienne's breathing steadied. She had encountered Shaiths before. Wraith-like entities twisted by darkness, lingering somewhere between angel and nightmare. She'd always thought they were a form of Fallen angel. Over the cycles, she'd learn they were *made* by the Fallen.

Shaiths were hunters. Trackers. And they never strayed far from their masters. In Xodom, everyone knew the Shaiths worked for two syndicate rulers: The Noirmother and the Ashqueen. By the sigils on the robes of these Shaiths, they seemed to be commanded by the Noirmother. Which meant her thief had bigger problems than just her.

Fabienne eased forward, careful to remain in the

shelter of darkness, her mind racing. If the Fraetèn—the crime syndicate led by the Noirmother—had sent Shaiths after him, then whatever trouble he was in, was deep. Which also meant *Zazràs* was tangled in something she hadn't anticipated. Did she still want to be involved with the heirloom?

She exhaled slowly. Yes. Yes she did. She would confront the thief and take the locket back.

Across from her, the shadows stirred. Fabienne caught a piece of conversation. It seemed her fellow thief was having a back and forth with the Shaith.

"As far as I'm concerned, you and the Fraetèn can piss off. I have nothing to do with the Noirmother and her syndicate," the thief said.

Rotting hèls. His voice.

She knew *that* voice.

It belonged to the one angel that made even the dusknite shudder.

Havoc.

Fabienne swallowed. She'd rarely crossed paths with him in the past. She'd heard plenty enough rumors. He was a Domenent with Pandemir ethèr. His powers enhanced his physical strength—turning any punch, stomp, or uppercut into such brutality, whatever was in his way would be utterly devastated. Like the revered and beloved Judge—Zhèmrazraèl Briyen, the Strong—Havoc could weaponize his brute force, becoming a physical battering ram, and something more devastating than any carved sword or spear. His body was the epitome of destruction, all on its own.

Burn it all! Why did the thief have to be him?

The Shaith answered Havoc.

"You will."

You will… what?

Fabienne's eyes snapped to abrupt movement just as a figure broke from the rooftop's edge, angelic wings snapping open as he launched into the air.

Havoc.

Fabienne moved. Her chase was wordless as she followed him through the skies, making sure to keep close so he wouldn't slip away. At first, he didn't know she was tracking him. At least, he seemed to be oblivious. But Fabienne knew the moment he sensed her. Havoc changed his flight pattern, beginning to maneuver away. He titled his head once, turning slightly to look behind him, as if confirming what he already suspected. The moment his eyes landed on her flying frame, he turned around, shot forward, and raced away from her.

But Fabienne was faster.

Havoc pulled away, but she gained on him quickly, weaving through the stone towers of Xodom with practiced ease. He had skill, but she had purpose. Rage lit her veins. Behind every wingbeat surged Tatiana's face, whole and healthy... for now. Her sisari lived on borrowed healing. If she didn't retrieve *Zazràs* and pay the blood debt soon—

She didn't let herself finish the thought.

Fabienne reached for her ethèr, pouring energy into her limbs, and into the powerful beat of her wings. The wind burned against her skin, the city a blur beneath them. She shot ahead, hand outstretched. Pushing harder, she leaned forward, reached for him—

He twisted at the last moment, dipping sharply beneath her grasp, his body rolling into a maneuver so tight she barely had time to adjust. Her momentum carried her forward as he banked hard to the left, diving low into the alleyways.

"Asheating—"

Fabienne cursed, adjusting her flight, folding her wings just enough to follow him into the narrow space between the buildings. The gap was tight, too tight for most to navigate at this speed, but she didn't slow, her focus locked onto his form a little ways in front of her.

She was so close, she could detail the trim along the edges of his leather boots. She pushed harder, ethèr crackling through her veins, propelling her with speed like a bolt of lightning. She was on him in an instant, matching his every movement, closing the distance.

Fabienne pulled up beside Havoc, and reached over. Her hand wrapped around his wrist. It was surprisingly warm and smooth. She flinched at the touch. At the arousal it sparked within her. Then the moment was gone—fleeting like starlight at the rise of a new dawn.

A shockwave of ethèr burst from him, powerful and unrestrained. The force of it sent a jolt up her arm, breaking her grip as light flared between them. And something else she couldn't quite understand. Fabienne gritted her teeth against the impact, her wings snapping wide to regain control just as he twisted in the air, flipping to face her mid-flight.

For the first time, she saw him up close.

Amber and honey eyes burned with mischief, framed by sharp features and the ghost of a smirk. His copper-red locs twisted in the wind while both sides of his head were cropped short and neat. His dark, ebony skin caught the rays of the city around them. His fitted leathers, adorned with buckles and belts, hinted at weapons he had yet to draw. Havoc's shoulders were broad, strong, his jawline hardened in a way that amplified his features. And for stars sake, that decadent mouth.

For a breath, neither of them moved.

Rotting. Burning. Hèls.

Havoc was a vision.

She'd known he was a brute. She'd heard the rumors about him for cycles. He was a merciless one at that. She didn't realize that he'd also be so rotting *beautiful.* She blinked, unable to keep from staring at him. With a small flicker of satisfaction, she noticed he was staring, too, his eyes growing molten.

Then he grinned. The sight nearly blinded her.

"Persistent little thief, aren't you?"

His voice was deep, triggering a shiver down her spine all the way to her toes. There was an easily disarming charm about him. An allure. It was deliciously tempting. And a hellish distraction.

Fabienne blinked, clearing her head. Then she lunged.

But Havoc was already moving. Wings unfurling, power crackling around him, he twisted out of reach, dropping into a sudden dive.

She followed him, refusing to let him escape.

Down, down, *down,* they went.

The city blurred. The buildings loomed. They were moments from colliding with the streets when he snapped his wings open, catching an updraft that sent him into a cutting arc. Fabienne matched him, their movements mirroring like a dance. Her hearts pounded, but she wasn't done.

She reached again, but this time, he was ready. He spun in midair, twisting toward her instead of away. The sudden reversal threw her off balance, and in the heartbeats it took to adjust, his hand brushed against her wrist. Her waist. He tugged her close, squeezing gently. Then he chuckled darkly, the sound curling around the winged curves of her ears.

Fabienne gasped. The touch was feather light.

Like a whisper.

Like a prayer.

Then he was gone.

Fabienne pulled up short, fury and exhilaration tangling in her chest as she spun, searching. He was already high above, silhouetted against the nightlùne, the locket dangling from his fingers. A bolt of rage leapt in her pulse at the sight of *Zazràs.* Havoc's baritone voice carried across the wind, teasing, rumbling through her chest.

"Better luck next time, my pretty little thief." Then he vanished into the dusknite.

CHAPTER 6
FABIENNE

Fabienne Evruel hovered for a long moment, ethèr coiling like vapor and snakes around her fists, and up the length of her arms. She wanted to scream. To rip the sky in half. Instead, she landed roughly on a flat, weathered rooftop, breath ragged. Her knees hit the stone and she stayed there, silent.

"What am I going to do? Burn you, Havoc! To the deepest dimensions of the Hèls."

Her blood debt was unpaid and now her payment was gone. The Ukaveli Syndicate, third in popularity, and brutality, to the Fraeten, would come for her to collect—and if they found her empty handed, they'd find Tatiana.

Fabienne rose slowly. She wiped the sweat from her brow, shot into the sky again, and turned east.

She needed that locket. It was the one form of payment the Ukaveli would accept.

She resolved to go after Havoc again. If she couldn't catch Havoc in the skies, she'd smoke him out on the ground. She unfurled her wings once more. The hunt wasn't over.

She had an inkling of where he might be headed. Either The Den of Ash or The Crying Veil. Ilk like him frequented both.

The fool probably didn't even know what *Zazràs* was. But since she'd made such an effort to get it, he'd determined to get involved. She'd never understand why. He should have left good and well alone. Her affairs were none of his business. He was probably bored and had nothing else to do. And somehow, without really trying, he'd gotten the best of her.

Twice.

Rage built in her chest. She forced it back down. She had to think. She took a breath, steadied herself, and looked around. While she was plotting, something about the dusknite had changed.

Fabienne leapt from rooftop to rooftop, wings drawn in close, cutting through the veil of midnight like a blade. She veered east at first, tracking what little residue of Havoc's ethèr remained—but it grew faint too quickly. Slippery.

She growled low in her throat and changed

direction, slicing across the rooftops and into Xodom's darker veins. The alleys here were narrower, the lights fewer. The ethèr was twisted down in these parts. Akin to the majik Fallen angels used. Signs were etched in Domènn, glowing softly on shuttered windows—wards to keep things out. Or in.

Here, where the buildings leaned too close and the air hung too still, Fabienne's flight slowed. She stretched her ethèr wide again searching for Havoc—and this time, she felt a knowing in her bones. She was being followed. And not by the Pandemir.

Shadows moved moments too late. There were brushes of wings where none should be. There was the tension of the predator now becoming prey. This wasn't just the echo of her own flight pattern. It was presence. Ominous and suffocating.

And there was more than one.

Her heartbeats stuttered once. Then leveled out. Fine. If an angel wanted her, let them come.

She dove down into the street and vanished between crumbling archways, slipping into the maze of Xodom's shady activity, rushing past Domenents dealing with their demons, where even light hesitated to enter.

There was one place she liked to go to disappear. The edge line of the Craven Wood. If she could slip out of the city's end undetected, she'd get there, then lie low for a little while.

She flew straight for Xodom's city limits where it began to merge into the Craven Wood.

The wood loomed ahead—thick black trees clawing skyward at the edge of the city, their bark like scorched bone, their roots splitting through the stone like tumors. Fabienne didn't stop. She darted beneath twisted branches, flying low beneath the canopy where the Wood had merged itself to the edge of Xodom, her wings brushing brambles that hissed as they grazed her.

Here, everything reeked of ancient curses. She hated the Craven Wood. But it was her best shot at shaking her pursuers, and she'd found it to be a great hiding spot when she needed to go dark.

For ten breaths, she flew.

For ten breaths, it worked.

Fabienne stopped short at the sight of a ripple in the night, followed by a glint of metal. A whisper of wings. She shot out of the canopy, and sauntered over low branches, desperately racing for the Wood. She came to an abrupt halt, mid-flight, backed into a cracked city square.

They weren't following her. They'd been herding her. Because they'd been waiting.

Fabienne looked around at the angels and wanted to curse. There were so many of them.

Not Sherèf. Not Watchers. Not Domenents. Not even mobsters.

They were Crescents. Every last one.

Hèls. Hèls. *Hèls.*

Over a dozen of them surrounded the square—perfectly poised, their eyes gleaming. The Transcendent assassins didn't have multicolored eyes like Domenents, instead their eyes had one hue with starry flecks, and for some reason that made their gaze all the more terrifying. They wore obsidian, form fitting leathers embroidered with the mark of the Fraetèn. They donned their weapons openly like jewels.

Fabienne wasn't a fool. Even if all they used were their hands, their bodies, their ethèr—that would be weapon enough. One Crescent smiled at her. A casual, patient, dangerous thing. Like a predator who'd finally cornered a prized animal.

"Void Reaver," another called, voice soft and cold. "Our Noirmother sends her regards."

Fabienne cursed, then pivoted, only to find her exit blocked by a dozen more Crescents.

No, no, *no.* This wasn't happening.

Her mind worked furiously. She could climb. Burst upward. Try to outrun them. Outfly them, even. But the space was tight. Her wings were cramped. Her breath came too fast. Her body was already worn from chasing Havoc. Still, she wouldn't go down without a fight.

Fabienne reached for her daggers, and in one fluid movement, launched herself at the closest Crescent. The impact was thunder and fire. Her blade caught his side, slicing clean through cloth and skin. He hissed and stumbled back. But in the same breath, he swiped a wing at her, sharp and bone-breaking like a newly forged battle staff. Another came from the right. Fabienne ducked low, pivoted, slammed her elbow into their ribs. Her ethèr surged through her limbs like liquid gold, sharpening her speed, her focus. She moved like lightning.

Two more charged.

She whirled, struck, spun in midair and slashed upward—one faltered. The other clipped her wing. She gritted her teeth against the pain and kept moving. But she was slowing.

There were too many.

A blade grazed her thigh. Another slammed the hilt of a sword into her ribs. She gasped, the pain slicing clean through her focus. She staggered.

That was all they needed.

From behind, a net of glowing ethèr flared open, casting a golden lattice across the alley. It snapped around her wings before she could spread them. The power burned into the membrane, locking them in place with a sickening crackle of dull light. Her knees hit the stone. The pain dropped her to one side. Her hands scrambled for her daggers again—but they were knocked away, spinning across the ground with metallic clangs.

Boots surrounded her. One stepped on her wrist, pressed hard, then cracked the bone. Fabienne snarled through her teeth, fighting hot tears, looking up at the Crescent who loomed over her with blank, expressionless eyes.

"You should've stayed in the shadows, little thief," he said quietly.

She spat blood onto the ground near his boot.

"Your manmèri should've swallowed a dagger," she hissed.

The Crescent raised his hand, his ethèr flaring bright. And brought it down. Light exploded behind her eyes. Something cracked. Everything went dark.

It took her a long time to come back. A feeling in her gut told her she'd been out too long.

Pain ebbed behind her eyes. Her wings were numb. Her body burned. Rough hands gripped her, hurling her around unceremoniously. Cold metal shackled her wrists. A dark hood was secured over her face. A thick, disgusting gag had been shoved into her mouth. All she could feel was motion—air swirling around her, the rush of wind, her body carried by flight. She didn't know where they were taking her. And still, no matter how hard she tried to get it back, *Zazràs* was still gone.

CHAPTER 7
EMMANUEL

The Den of Ash was alive with heat, laughter, and the thick scent of burning candles mingled with spilled wine. Lanterns hung from fraying ropes, casting golden glows over warped tables, mismatched chairs, and angels who didn't care what their rank was so long as the drinks kept flowing. Emmanuel Alfonse sat back in his chair, half-listening to the conversations around him, nursing the last sip of his drink.

The job had gone sideways. Reaver wasn't supposed to have noticed him. Let alone find him and follow him. Even when he was surrounded by Shaiths, she hadn't flinched. Her eyes were for him. He almost laughed at that. He wasn't one to shy away from attention, but hers was unnerving. It stirred things in him that didn't make sense.

But none of that mattered to him now. He'd stolen *Zazràs* and out-flew one of the best thieves he'd ever seen. The only problem was, he'd hardly gotten the rotting thing tucked into his belt before his rotting name began dragging through Xodom's streets, alerting every bounty hunter in the city.

Yolanda had warned him to get rid of the locket. She'd said there were many who'd stop at nothing to get it. But Emmanuel didn't care. If he was going to get rid of *Zazràs*, it would be for a high price. He had immunity to buy, and *Zazràs* would be what bought it for him.

This dusknite, he wouldn't let himself think too much about any of it. Right here, right now, he was just another rogue with a drained bottle, an empty goblet, and a little time to kill before deciding his next move. Emmanuel grew distracted, watching the flow of angels coming in and out of the tavern, floating past him absentmindedly.

That is, until *she* sat down across from him.

The aèl was stunning. Her deep brown skin seemed to iridesce under the tavern's dim glow. Her eyes were dark, one like midnight and the other like a silver star. And that smile. Full, luscious, promising all kinds of trouble.

The female angel had his attention, and she knew it. His nostrils flared as his gaze lazily slithered down her curvaceous frame, memorizing every detail. The aèl's fitted silks suggested privilege, but not so much that she stood out as a target. No, she had the look of an angel who belonged here. An angel who thrived in places like this. And right now, she was interested in him.

Emmanuel smirked, tilting his glass toward her. “Now what’s a pretty thing like you doing in a place like this?”

She leaned forward, resting her chin in her hand, her fingers grazing the rim of his empty glass.

"Not too much this dusknite." Her eyelashes fluttered, making Emmanuel's six hearts skip three beats. "Looking for good company. Maybe a little excitement."

Her voice curled in the air like incense—slow, warm, and seductive.

Emmanuel arched a brow, studying her. There was a calculated smoothness in her voice, the kind that slithered past an aèn’s defenses before the male even realized what was happening. He had heard tones like that before—temptation wrapped in silk. Only problem was, there was usually a dagger laced in traitorous poison hidden in there, too. A warning flared in his mind, but he suppressed it. If she wanted to play, he would oblige.

Typically, no one sought him out for company

unless they wanted something. No one ever spoke to him this way unless there was a reason. One that usually ended with him on the run or off on another hunt. And yet, he found himself intrigued, tilting his head as he lazily spun the empty glass between his fingers, lightly brushing the tips of hers.

"Excitement, huh? You chose the wrong place, pretty one. Here has nothing but wasted angels and old regrets to offer you."

The aèl grinned, slow and knowing. "Maybe I'm looking for the kind of trouble only an aèn like you can offer."

Hers eyes flashed. His hearts danced. She was fire, and he wanted to burn. Trouble like her always introduced itself with a smile. But it had been a long dawn, she was so rotting beautiful, and stars knew how long it'd been since he let himself have a bit of fun.

Emmanuel decided to play along.

"Why don't we find somewhere quiet where we can cause a little—" Emmanuel breathed the words close to her winged ear. "—trouble."

She grinned, rising, and taking him by the hand. The aèl led him to a private chamber that was dimly lit, just enough to cast long shadows against the walls. She led him inside, her movements slow, deliberate, a meandering stroll down the hedonistic lanes of the

Hèls. Emmanuel let himself enjoy every single moment. He thought of how he'd fold her wings, and then her body, beneath him, as they had his idea of a good time. His instincts hummed in warning, but he was enthralled by her.

The scent of angel-wine was fainter here. Stronger now was the metallic bite of cold steel—the kind you only noticed if you were used to dodging it. The door clicked shut. The air changed. Bright, searing light exploded across the chamber. Emmanuel flinched, momentarily blinded as his senses screamed a warning. Then he heard it. Wings unfolding. Boots shifting. Steel laced in ethèr surfacing.

Rotting hèls.

His vision cleared just in time to see angels. Too many to count. They were armed and smiling.

He'd floated straight into a trap.

His body moved before his brain did—reflexes honed from a thousand near-death experiences snapping into action. The first blade came for his throat.

Emmanuel twisted, ducking low as the blade whistled past his ear. He lashed out with his own dagger, forcing his attacker back, wings snapping open to propel him across the room. The aèl who seduced him was gone—her job had been expertly done. And now, he was left alone with a throng of armed enforcers. Emmanuel caught the brands on their necks.

Stars.

They were all Fraetèn.

They came at him from all sides, but he was faster. He moved like smoke, slipping between their attacks, countering when he could, avoiding when he couldn't. His Pandemir ethèr flared, enhancing his reflexes, his physical strength, turning every strike into fatal blows. Except each hit he landed only slowed his attackers, it didn't put them down permanently.

Emmanuel cursed, trying to focus so he could get enough leverage to get the rot out of here. But the Fraetèn wouldn't let up. Their blows were heavy. Precision-trained. Designed both to kill, and to break.

A sharp crack exploded against his ribs as the hilt of a heavy sword slammed into his side. He gasped, staggering, barely managing to avoid the second hit aimed at his skull. Golden blood dripped down his leathers, hot and sticky. Too much of it belonged to him. He had to get out of here *now*.

But he was surrounded.

Emmanuel faltered—just a fraction of a second. It was more than enough for the Fraetèn to capitalize on. Hands grabbed him. Then there was a blow to the back of his knees. Another to his jaw. His vision blurred, his strength draining as they struck again, and again—

A voice cut through the haze. Smooth. Amused.

"Well, well. This is our infamous Vagabond. I will say, for a Pandemir, I expected more."

Emmanuel groaned as he was hauled upright, forced to kneel as boots clicked against the wooden floor.

Hèls. Just his luck. It was a Crescent.

The assassin crouched before him, dark amusement gleaming in her ember colored eyes.

"Took your time," Emmanuel sputtered, golden blood gushing from his teeth.

The Crescent smirked. Emmanuel wanted to spit in her eyes. "I like to let my prey wear themselves out first." She reached forward, tapping Emmanuel's thigh. "And would you look at that. *Zazràs*."

The locket was ripped from him before he could react. The Crescent held it up to the light, examining the ivory stone at its center.

"I'll admit, I was curious why you risked so much for this. Especially knowing the attention it would attract. Now I see why." Her eyes fell to Emmanuel, a deep malice hovering at the surface. Her grip tightened. "It's a shame you got caught. The Fallen would happily bargain if it meant freeing one of their own. You probably could've paid your bloodline debt with this." A cruel grin. "Well. The Noirmother will certainly be pleased."

Emmanuel gave a weak chuckle, though he felt no joy. The knowledge of the Crescent about his debt was a blow he wasn't expecting. No one knew about his debt to the Fallen. Or so he thought. He looked up at her as blood dripped into his eyes.

"Glad I could be of service. Do Crescents fancy a good negotiation, too? I'd like to bargain you out of those fatigues."

The Crescent looked at him for a brief moment. Then her fist, covered in brass knuckles, collided with his jaw, his nose, and his temples, sending him sprawling deep into the dark.

CHAPTER 8

EMMANUEL

Emmanuel drifted in and out of consciousness. The first thing he made sense of was airborne movement. He found that he was in a cage connected to the bottom of a chariot. The Fraetèn were carrying him like some kind of wild animal. The degradation of it all astounded him. He was balled up and chained. Most of all, he was humiliated at what had happened to him.

Yolanda warned him this would happen. He had been so arrogant, so confident only the dusknite before. Stupid. He was so burning stupid. Now he was paying for it with regret.

The cage rattled around him, suspended beneath the winged transport. His wrists and ankles were bound in reinforced steel, and his wings—his rotting wings—were locked in place. The only consolation was they hadn't Clipped him. Yet.

Pain pulsed through the joints where oversized metal clamps bit into his skin, muting his ethèr. He drew on his powers, trying to pull out the Pandemir strength from within. Nothing. Not even a sputter. The Fraetèn had finally caught him. And they'd chained him, and his ethèr, like a rabid beast.

He shifted slightly, groaning against the pain that coiled in his ribs. The stolen heirloom was gone. His leverage was gone. He had nothing now but grit and time, and maybe not much of that either. The realization sent a slow, simmering rage through his bones. He had spent cycles outrunning them. Dodging their reach. And now? A single job. A single mistake. And they had him in their grip.

Through the haze, he heard the Crescent's voice.

"Take him straight to the Noirmother. She's requested the Vagabond be delivered to her directly."

The chariot shifted, banking hard. They were heading deeper into Fraetèn territory. Emmanuel closed his eyes and exhaled slowly. He needed a plan. Fast. Because if they brought him to the Noirmother, he wasn't flying out alive.

As Emmanuel plotted, he noticed the chariot ride began stretching longer than he expected. That meant two things: either they were taking him to the

Pits or the Noirmother was somewhere else deep in the territory. He swallowed. What did the Fraetèn Boss have in mind?

The air was thin, the high-altitude pressure pressing against his skull. He tested the cuffs around his wrists, feeling the bite of cold steel against his skin. His ethèr was weakened, barely a flicker beneath the reinforced chains binding his wings and limbs. He hated it. Hated the feeling of being caged, even within his own blood and fôrs.

The Fraetèn angels flying the chariot didn't speak much, but Emmanuel caught the occasional glance between them. Tension. Uncertainty. Something wasn't right.

The Crescent's voice cut through the silence.

"You look too comfortable, Vagabond."

Emmanuel lifted his head lazily, offering a crooked grin despite the pain throbbing in his face, limbs, and all across his ribs. "I'd be more comfortable with a drink." A pause. "And a long dusknite with you."

The Crescent smirked. Then a shocking bolt of energy cracked through his bones. Emmanuel wanted to scream. But he wouldn't give them the satisfaction. He grit his teeth against the pain, panting when relief finally came. The Crescent continued on smoothly.

"You should be praying, Vagabond."

"Angels like me don't pray, oh devilish one."

A snort. "Oh, you'll start." A slow, crawling grin. "I promise."

He turned away. Then he saw it.

Through the slats of the chariot's side panels, a figure was being dragged through the clouds in a cage like his. Emmanuel frowned when he sensed, no, *felt* something familiar. It took him a moment to realize what it was. He felt *her*. The ripple of her familiar ethèr slipped into his cage. It wasn't strong—but it was hers.

Reaver.

Burning stars.

So. They'd caught her, too.

As the chariot surged deeper into the sky, Emmanuel couldn't shake the silence in the air.

It wasn't the kind of silence that came from exhaustion or duty. It was heavy. Oppressive. Hopeless. The kind of silence that pressed in around you like a prelude to something monstrous. Even the Fraetèn—two battle-worn angels flanking the Crescent—had stopped speaking entirely. One wouldn't meet Emmanuel's gaze. The other kept checking his restraints often.

Emmanuel adjusted his weight, testing the manacles again. They didn't budge. These cuffs were designed to hold angels stronger than him. Probably of Higherank, too. Which meant whoever had ordered them knew exactly what Emmanuel was capable of. And that chilled him more than he wanted to admit.

He glanced sideways through the iron slats of the chariot's transport cage. The clouds outside were darker now, almost bruised. A faint violet sparkle pulsed through them like veins under skin. Storms weren't common this high up. Not unless conjured.

The Crescent had said the Noirmother wanted him delivered to her personally. Emmanuel had danced through Fraetèn fire before. He'd never been dumb enough to be in their debt, though. He'd worked with them before, until they double-crossed him for coin and power. Never had they made this much effort for a regular job. And it wasn't even their job anyway, so why were they involved?

What you stole from the aèl belongs to them.

He wondered how long he would curse himself for being so stupid. For getting caught up in this twisted mess with the Fraetèn. He'd wanted to screw around with Reaver and break her impenetrable reputation around Xodom—*not* get kidnapped by one of the most ruthless syndicates in the Megalopolis. There was all of this ceremony. All of these dramatics. And for what?

Zazràs.

That cursed locket. The moment he'd touched it, the moment he'd felt the heartbeat pulsing through its center stone, he knew it was more than an heirloom. More than a weapon. But he'd thought it was something he could easily trade for power. Maybe he'd even buy his way out of Xodom altogether, go somewhere entirely different, and live out the rest of his life... far away from the Fallen hunting him.

Instead, burning Shaiths came for him.

He flexed his hands again, blood crusting on his knuckles. The Fraetèn wouldn't keep him caged. He was too valuable. He knew too much. Had seen too much. They would interrogate him. Study him. Beat him over and over in the attempts to break him. Then when they realized he wouldn't break, they would have him Clipped, siphoned, and killed permanently, stripping him from being able to enter the Ellelights like all angels when their fôrs is ready to cross over.

He cursed himself again for not heeding Yolanda's warning. He slumped back against the cold steel bars, letting his eyes flutter half-shut. Not because he was tired. But because stillness helped him think.

He couldn't die. Not yet.

The chariot dipped suddenly, and for the first time, Emmanuel caught a glimpse of what lay below. A tower. No—worse. A spire, built into the bones of a cliffside, rising like a spear between cracked rock and steaming ash vents. Its windows were narrow slits. Its outer walls glowed faintly with majik, marked with sigils he didn't recognize.

Burning hèls.

They'd brought him all the way to the Fraetèn Sanctum. *Rot.* How was he going to get out?

His breath hitched.

Most of the city didn't even know the Fraetèn had places like this. Hidden prisons and strongholds built in the seams of Xodom, where angels were unmade and forgotten. You didn't leave these places. You didn't escape. There was one way in, and no way out.

The Crescent stood, her voice calm. "I'll show you a bit of mercy and give you one warning. You'll behave when you meet the Noirmother. Or she'll break you, until being a good dog is branded into your brain and bones. If you don't want to be taught how to play fetch, I suggest you shut up and not bark."

Emmanuel spat a clot of blood onto the floor at the assassin's boots. "Piss off, asheater."

The Crescent's eyes gleamed. Then she shrugged. "Can't say I didn't warn you."

The chariot locked into its landing rig with a jolt that rattled Emmanuel's skull. He gritted his teeth, bracing himself as the doors creaked open. Warm air hit him—thick and sour, like rotting flowers and burnt copper. Something wrong lived in that place.

Two Fraetèn reached in, grabbing his arms. His wing-locks flared, searing his nerves as they dragged him from the cage. His boots scraped the metal. The pain was brittle and white-hot. As they hauled him toward the tower doors, he looked up once more.

The sky above Xodom had never looked so far away.

CHAPTER 9

FABIENNE

Fabienne sat motionless, her wrists bound behind her. The cold bite of steel pressed against her skin. The sharp sting of ethèr-forged cuffs dug into her wrists, disrupting the natural rhythm of her power. Her wings, sealed in place by the Fraetèn's cursed shackles, ached like severed limbs. Struggling would be useless. The Fraetèn weren't amateurs.

Her breath came slow. She decided to focus on something more valuable than resistance.

She started listening.

The chariot rattled as it soared through the air. The vessel's curved floor sloped beneath her with each turn and rise. She mapped their flight progression in silence, calculating twists and turns in direction, descent angles, and wind velocity. Every tilt was a clue. Every jolt a piece of invaluable information she could use later on.

The Fraetèn spoke freely, convinced of her helplessness. Some boasted about how easily she'd been taken. Others speculated over the price the Noirmother might put on her wings, if the Fraetèn Boss didn't decide to keep her wings as a trophy. One voice murmured something lower, almost hesitant.

"You think she'll keep this one?"

A scoff.

"She'd have to survive. By the looks of it..." A pause. Then. "She won't."

Fabienne ground her teeth, her fury curling hot. Then a Crescent was called. She froze.

Crescents weren't ordinary angels. They were executioners. Elite assassins forged in blood and shadow, trained to make death an art. Not to mention they were Higheranks. While all the angels present were Domenents, Crescent angels were of Transcendent rank. That alone made them lethal. Fabienne had never in her life been so foolish as to underestimate a Crescent. If one had been assigned to her, it meant one thing.

This had never been a simple capture. It had been orchestrated with precision—every movement, every flight planned long before she even realized she had been marked. Crescents didn't just stumble upon their prey. They hunted with intent, waiting for the perfect moment to strike. A Crescent meant she wasn't just a target. She wasn't some unfortunate thief caught in the wrong place at the wrong time. They'd been watching her for a long time. Which meant the Noirmother had plans for her.

Her stomach twisted. Was all of this connected to *Zazràs*? Or was there more to them kidnapping her? After all, she was in debt to the Ukaveli Syndicate, *not* the Fraetèn. So what in the hèls did they want with her?

The chariot gave a violent jolt. They were landing. Fabienne counted her breaths. Ten. Twenty. Thirty. Then the wheels screeched against stone. Rough hands seized her, yanking her forward. Her boots scraped against the floor as she was hoisted out of the chariot, her bound wings screaming with pain at the sudden movement. The bag over her head muffled sound, but not enough to block the crude jokes exchanged between the Fraetèn.

"Think she'll beg?" one sneered.

"Nah," another chuckled. "Noirmother likes it better when they break."

A third voice was more thoughtful. "She doesn't look like the type to break. Not easily."

Fabienne's jaw tightened, but she made no sound. She would *not* break.

The air shifted as they passed through a threshold—cooler, heavier. The scent of old metal, scorched stone, and sulfur filled her lungs. Her skin prickled. Wherever they were, it wasn't a surface-level compound. This place was old. Ancient.

They descended down steps. Then another turn. Another hall. Left one time. Down three steps. Right. Down a slope. She memorized it all. Every turn. Every shift. Every moment. This was her currency. Her future escape.

With thought, Fabienne realized they weren't taking her to a cell. The walls breathed differently here—thicker, denser, like the shadows themselves were alive. Somewhere in the distance, she heard the low hum of furnaces. The rhythmic hiss of gates opening and closing. A place built for secrecy. And silence.

When the Fraetèn stopped, her pulse quickened. Then the bag was ripped from her head.

Light flooded her vision, harsh and golden, but Fabienne did not flinch. She had trained herself for this. She would show no weakness. No fear. She took in her surroundings at once.

She was in a vast chamber. Carved of obsidian-veined stone, lit by lanterns suspended on iron chains, each flame flickering like molten fire. Massive winged statues loomed from alcoves, each one grotesque—

angelic and monstrous at once. This was no throne room. This was a sanctum. But the Fraetèn didn't believe in kings. Instead, they built their own gods.

And at the center, lounging like a Konda serpent coiled on its perch, was Noirmother Alexandria Nafariel. She sat in a high-backed chair of polished onyx, wings stretched wide behind her—feathered and gleaming like metallic gray plumes that faded into bright silver halfway down the feathers, casting long, claw-shaped shadows across the floor. She wore no crown. She needed none.

With a shift of the Noirmother's movement, Fabienne caught sight of an extra set of wings. Then it all clicked. Feathered wings. Seven wing pairs. The Crescents.

She almost fell over.

The Fraetèn around her were all Domenents, but the Noirmother was no such thing.

Noirmother Alexandria was a Transcendent.

Fabienne wanted to fight the air. That knowledge infinitely complicated things. No wonder the Fraetèn employed the force of Crescents. They were of the same rank.

The Noirmother's skin was the color of burnished chestnut, smooth and warm like a sumyrin dawn. Her emerald eyes glowed faintly, never blinking. Her coiled hair was pulled back in a thick crown-like braid, shot through with evergreen threads and tiny bone charms. And on her rouge lips was a smile carved with cruelty.

"Fabienne Evruel."

Fabienne tensed. No one ever spoke her true name aloud. Few even knew it. She caught the flicker of surprise across several faces in the court chamber. The Noirmother spoke her name like a possession. Fabienne swallowed down her rising bitterness. She squared her shoulders, lifted her chin. She didn't respond.

The Noirmother's lips curled. "I expected more of a fight."

Fabienne met her gaze. "What would be the point?"

A low chuckle rumbled from the Noirmother. Silky. Rich. Laced with quiet, brutal power.

"They did tell me you were a smart one." She waved a hand. "Bring in the other one."

Fabienne tensed. The court doors slammed open. Another captive was dragged inside.

Fabienne gasped as she stared at Havoc. He was bruised. Bloodied. His wings were bound. But somehow, he was still grinning. That stupid, maddening, infuriating grin.

Fabienne's stomach clenched.

The Noirmother's smile was serpentine. "I believe you've already met Emmanuel Alfonse."

Havoc looked awful. Dried blood crusted along his jaw. His lip was split. One of his wings looked partially dislocated. But his eyes burned with the same mischief he'd had when he'd stolen *Zazràs* out from under her.

"Well met, my pretty little thief," he drawled, voice hoarse. "Did you miss me?"

Fabienne clenched her fists. This blasted idiot. None of this would be happening right now if it wasn't for him. She wanted to throttle him. The Fraetèn forced him to his knees beside her. Fabienne glared at him.

"*You*," she spat.

"Me," he grinned back, tilting his head in amusement.

"I will have your wings for this," Fabienne seethed.

"You'll have to get in line." His grin only stretched.

She wanted to reach over and carve it off his face. Marred as it was, he was still so rotting beautiful. It made her blood boil even more.

One of the Fraetèn stepped forward, something gleaming in his hand. *Zazràs*. Fabienne's breath caught. The locket pulsed faintly in the low light. The air itself seemed to tremble around it. Alive. Calling. The Fraetèn held it up like a trophy.

"He had it," he said. "Took it off him after Jenessa delivered him to us."

The Noirmother's gaze lingered on the relic. "Interesting." Then, slowly, she looked between Fabienne and Emmanuel. "Quite the mess you two have made."

Fabienne could barely breathe. Her chest burned. She had to get it back. She had to get out. Tatiana's life depended on it. She lunged. Or tried to.

The moment she moved, the blow came—piercing, immediate. A vicious strike slammed into her face, the force snapping her head to the side with a crack. Searing-hot pain exploded along her cheekbone. She staggered, barely catching herself before she hit the stone.

The court chamber went still. The burning in her skull was nothing compared to the roar of emotion inside her. She tasted blood. Rage. Defeat. But she didn't cry out. She didn't look away. She wanted them to see her. Broken or not, bleeding or not—she would *not* look away. Beside her, Havoc stirred slightly. Not enough to provoke a response from the watching Fraetèn. But enough to glance her way. His face—still bloodied, swollen—shifted just a fraction. She didn't know what she saw there.

Respect?

Recognition?

None of it mattered.

Zazràs pulsed again in the corner of her vision. She needed it back.

If she didn't pay her debt, Tatiana wouldn't just get sick again. She would be executed. Quietly and without a trace. Because that was how the Ukaveli Syndicate handled unfinished contracts.

Fabienne's mind spiraled—back to the dusk she'd signed the vow. She remembered the smell of incense and iron ink, the slice of the dagger across her palm as she cut herself open and sealed the blood mark that indebted her. She'd floated before a table of masked angels and promised her life if they spared, if they *saved*, her sisari's. If they'd give her a cure for Tatiana, she'd give them her life. They held up their end of the bargain, and she held up hers.

That vow had followed her into every job since. Every heist. Every sleepless dawn. Until she wanted out after cycles of successful jobs. She worked hard to pay off her debt and they said *no*.

But Fabienne had been smart. She'd been listening. And on her last job, she learned the Ukaveli Boss wanted *Zazràs*. First one to bring it to him would have all their debts cleared. She'd planned and plotted.

And failed.

Because now? She was here. Bound. Battered. With the locket right there—dangling in front of her like a joke. A cruel, malevolent joke. All thanks to this stars-forsaken, asheating, Pandemir. The Noirmother watched, almost bored.

Fabienne wanted to scream. Instead, she breathed. Slow. Measured. Just enough to keep her from drowning in her own fury. Her gaze locked back onto *Zazràs*. It was a curse. A tether to something old and powerful. It would change the balance of power across Xodom. It was also her way out of the Ukaveli's tight grip.

Her gaze snapped sideways again to Havoc. He was watching the Noirmother. Calm and calculated, his smirk disappeared as he watched her, like a predator biding his time. In that moment, Fabienne thought maybe, just maybe, he was more than just a good looking idiot.

The Noirmother finally leaned forward. The Fraetèn tensed. Fabienne's body followed suit, every one of her joints locked and taut like a bowstring.

"Now that we are all here," Noirmother Alexandria said, voice like velvet scraping over bone, "I have a job for you two."

CHAPTER 10
FABIENNE

"A job."

Fabienne spoke the words tentatively, not wanting to draw the Noirmother's ire. The court chamber was deathly quiet as she wrestled with her thoughts. What could this monster of an angel possibly want her to do? And how would this get her out of her debt with the Ukaveli Syndicate? Another thought settled into her mind.

"A job for *us*." She threw a pointed look at Havoc who simply gave her that stupid grin of his. And he winked at her. The piece of rot actually *winked*. "What are you on about Noirmother?"

Noirmother Alexandria smiled. She was a beautiful angel. The same way a blade was before it slit across your throat.

"Leave it to you to ask all the right questions, Fabienne."

Fabienne held her tongue, not falling for the bait. She listened, seeing if she could pick apart anything of importance from what the Noirmother would say.

"You are in debt to the Ukaveli, yes?"

Fabienne tensed. The way the Boss spoke the name of the syndicate she was in debt to was almost like uttering a curse.

"And you procured this stone," she waved a hand, and *Zazràs* floated above her palm. "So you could pay it off. Correct?"

Fabienne's cheeks flushed. Before she could answer, Havoc cut in.

"What's your burning point, queen of devils?"

Fabienne sucked in a sharp gasp as the Crescent to her right flickered a hand. The assassin didn't move. But Havoc's entire body jerked. He grit his teeth against unrelenting pain as he writhed on the stone floor, his body contorting in odd angles. Fabienne felt bad for him. But not enough to ask the Noirmother to intervene.

When satisfied he'd suffered enough, Noirmother Alexandria rose a hand. Immediately the Crescent stopped, and Havoc fell limp to the floor, before the Fraetèn dragged him upright to his knees. A coiling rage flickered in his eyes as he looked at the Fraetèn Boss, but he said nothing.

"If you went for the locket, it lets me know you have some knowledge about valuable relics. Some as old as time."

Fabienne's lips pressed into a thin line. What was she getting at? Fabienne knew about all kinds of relics. Lockets, stones, gems, blades. None of it mattered to her if it couldn't be used to pay her rotting debt.

"Permission to say a word, Noirmother," Fabienne said, testing her shackled liberty.

The Fraetèn shifted. A Crescent opened their palm. Fabienne prepared for the blow. But it never came. She blinked, and found the Noirmother had raised her hand. Fabienne almost sighed out loud.

"Speak, child."

"I am... *studious* in old relics. Yes. Those belonging to angels, giants, even the fae. But what does that have to do with anything? With all due respect, I owe you no debt. My qualms lie with the Ukaveli. Why am I here?"

The Noirmother studied Fabienne a long while. So long, Fabienne thought for sure she was leaving the court chamber in a coffin. Then the Fraetèn Boss spoke.

"You are correct. You are one of few who owe me

no debt. But you're the Ukaveli's best thief. And there's something I need that only you can steal. My thieves have tried." A pause. "They're all dead. I need *you.*" Her gaze flickered to Havoc, who was still glaring at her. "And the Vagabond, too, of course. You have brains, but he has strength. Together, you will not fail me."

Noirmother Alexandria Nafariel spoke with the ease of a Roièssa, her emerald eyes glinting as she leaned forward, fingers tapping idly on the arm of her high-backed chair. The weight of her presence pressed into the chamber like a thick fog—suffocating those who dared challenge her.

A snort rang out from beside Fabienne. She almost groaned at the same moment another blow landed to he back of Havoc's head. Unable to control herself, Fabienne blurted out.

"Have you not had enough? Or will you keep pressing until you're killed?"

Havoc, Vagabond and fool, was making things worse. He met her gaze, something dark coloring those molten eyes, before turning to the Noirmother.

"Pray tell, Noirmother," Havoc drawled, smirking through the golden blood pooling down the side of his face. "Is this where we thank you? For hindering us from paying former debts while shackling us to new ones?"

One of the Fraetèn moved without warning—a brutal backhanded strike. Havoc's head snapped to the side, a fresh line of blood trailing from his mouth. He let out a low chuckle, shaking his head as though the hit had merely been an inconvenience.

Fabienne clenched her fists behind her back. Idiot. Blasted, blood boiling, idiot.

The Noirmother blinked, studying Emmanuel like he was some Bloodhyena she couldn't quite understand. "You really don't know when to hush, do you child?"

Havoc grinned through the pain, lifting a shoulder in a lazy half-shrug. "It's a gift."

Fabienne wanted to kick him. Instead, she kept her gaze forward, jaw tight. She had to focus on the plan. Not him.

The Noirmother continued, ignoring Havoc entirely. "The Fraetèn are not the only power in Xodom, nor the only ones who command respect in the megalopolis. There are others—less refined, more desperate—who seek what does not belong to them."

She gestured slightly, and a Crescent stepped forward, unrolling a parchment filled with names, symbols, and crude markings. Fabienne's eyes flicked over it, catching the sigils of at least five different mobs. Some well-known, others only spoken of in whispered warnings. She noticed one of the names was Ashqueen Khadijah. Fabienne could have passed out. No one in Xodom's history had ever been bold enough to go head-to-head with the queen of all Crescents. Was the Noirmother mad? This could trigger civil war.

The Fraetèn Boss leaned back, clasping her hands. "There is a relic in existence that every syndicate in Xodom desires, one that has been lost for more than an Age but has now been... found."

Holy, burning stars. Fabienne knew where this was going. Havoc's head snapped up. His eyes narrowed at the Boss, his lips bowing in a deep frown. So, he knew where this was going, too.

"The two of you will hunt down, find, and procure for me the stone called Désakré."

Fabienne's jaw hung.

Désakré.

She had heard whispers of it before. There were ample legends of a sacred stone tied to the Etherien stars themselves, rumored to hold unbreakable power. The first Domenent who wielded it was said to bend all worship and piety to her will. Whoever held it could tip the balance of power between all angels, both Etherien and Fallen.

"Where in the burning hèls is Désakré?" Havoc spat.

When the blow didn't come, Fabienne found herself loosing a tight breath on his behalf.

The Noirmother smiled. A sweet, cunning, deadly thing.

"In the grave of a Taétàn king."

“No,” Fabienne breathed.

The Noirmother raised an eyebrow, watching her knowingly. Havoc burst out laughing. It was all Fabienne could do to *not* crawl on top of him and stomp him in his face.

“The grave of a Taétàn king?” He cracked his neck from side to side, without a flinch for the pain he must be feeling. Fabienne's envy of his strength and willpower was a nauseating thing she wanted to crush by embedding her dagger into his skull. “So this is a suicide mission.”

Fabienne ignored him. She only had eyes for the Fraetèn Boss.

The Noirmother exhaled, as if she'd expected this response.

“If you refuse, then you are of no use to me.”

Something shifted at Fabienne's right. A signal. Then the doors at the edge of the chamber opened. Two Shaiths glided in, dragging something behind them. No—*someone*. Fabienne’s stomach twisted as the figure was thrown forward—a mangled wreck of what had once been an angel. She recognized him. Or at least, she recognized what was left of him.

"Oh my—" Fabienne whispered. "Jeduriel?"

The thief, Jeduriel, grunted. His wings—what remained of them—were charred, twisted things with the talons broken, snapped and hanging, with large metals rings piercing through his wings. He'd been Clipped. His body bore marks of unimaginable torment. Jagged lashes split his skin open. His halo had been shattered, and the remains fused into the burns on his back. The scent of brimstone clung to the air around him, sickening and wrong.

Fabienne stilled.

Havoc fell deathly quiet.

Jeduriel groaned, scarcely conscious, his head tilting upward just enough to look at them. And despite everything—despite his shattered body, despite the agony carved into his bones... There was still a flicker of life in his eyes. A flash of defiance remained.

Then the Crescent behind the Noirmother opened her hand, summoned her ethèr, and began siphoning his fôrs. It was a simple motion. A flick of her fingers. A projection of ethèr. Jeduriel contorted, screaming as his body writhed on the floor. A golden spirit with an ivory silhouette slipped from the center of his chest, before turning into a white, flame. The

Crescent pulled his fôrs to her palm. And without ceremony, crushed it into nothing. Jeduriel's body tumbled to the stone with a crack, lifeless.

Fabienne's stomach lurched. The silence that followed was suffocating. She blinked hard, fury and terror colliding in her chest. Havoc shuffled on his feet beside her. A muscle in his jaw flexed. His body was still, but his fingers twitched. Not with fear. But rage.

Fabienne and Havoc shared a look between them.

She found her own terror mirrored in his eyes.

"You understand now, don't you?" Noirmother Alexandria cooed. "What happens when you refuse me?"

Fabienne's mind was reeling.

Désakré.

If it was as powerful as they claimed... Could she use it? For herself. For her sisari. To pay the debt. To reclaim everything they'd lost.

She turned to Havoc again. There was understanding in his gaze, but also cold calculation, and deep beneath that, distrust. He was thinking the same thing she was. What Désakré could do? What the other would do to keep it from them?

A silent agreement formed between them. But so did a silent threat. If he got to the stone first, he'd take it. If she got to it first, it was hers.

The Noirmother smiled, sensing the accord. She stood, graceful as an ancient queen.

"We will outfit you," she said, "with passage, weapons, and instructions. You will infiltrate Takari, the home of those stars-forsaken giants. You will locate the tomb of their Taétàn king in their catacombs. And you will bring me Désakré." She stepped down from the dais, stopping between them.

"You have one wèk," she said softly. "Fail me, and you'll learn what it means for an angel to be unmade."

CHAPTER 11

FABIENNE

"Time to move."

Fabienne and Emmanuel were yanked to their feet—not harshly, but firmly, like assets being relocated rather than prisoners. The chain binding Fabienne's wrists scraped as it shifted, ethèr locks pulsing with low, static hums. She didn't resist, but her mind whirred. She tactically noted exit routes, memorized faces, mapped the angles of the chamber in case anything changed. She catalogued weapons, which Fraetèn had heavier breathing, and which of them leaned on bad knees. One Fraetèn wore a bandage beneath his leathers—a weakness. She memorized it all.

They were led down a dim corridor branching off from the sanctum. The air here was drier, dustier. There were no windows. Only flickering ethèr lanterns mounted in alcoves, throwing dancing shadows across faded murals etched into the stone. Xodom's dark history had been carved into its bones. There were depictions of angelic betrayals, executions, forgotten kings and the rise of mobsters. Fabienne frowned grimly at the sight.

The Fraetèn said nothing as they floated down the halls. Their silence unnerved her more than any of their threats. Eventually, they stopped at an iron gate. One of the Fraetèn knocked twice, then pressed her palm to a sigil embedded in the wall. The gate groaned open, revealing a narrow passage lit by violet flame. A new chamber waited beyond.

Weapons racks lined the walls—some locked, some open. Several sets of armor stood on display, styled with Fraetèn markings and cuts built for mobility and stealth. In the center stood a long obsidian table, its surface bare.

One of the Fraetèn grunted. "Wait here."

They stepped out and closed the door behind them with a thud that echoed too long. Emmanuel leaned back against the table, exhaling sharply through his nose.

"Nice place," he appraised, looking around. "Bit much on the dramatics."

Fabienne didn't answer. She didn't even look at him. She crossed to the other side of the chamber and sat on the stony floor, wings locked, spine straight. She closed her eyes. She needed to focus. To think of a way to escape this foolish quest. But Havoc's voice cut through the quiet anyway.

"You hate the Taétàn, huh?"

Her eyes snapped open. He was watching her—head tilted, still bleeding, but studying her like he was trying to decipher a riddle scrawled in fading ink. Fabienne scowled.

"You went rigid, then pale when the Noirmother mentioned them. Thought you'd explode."

"Mind your business, and I'll mind mine," she said sweetly.

Havoc held her gaze. "Whether you like it or not, we're in this together now. So actually, it *is* my business." A pause. Then, he added, "Just know, I don't trust them, and I definitely don't trust you."

"Good," Fabienne replied cooly. At least they were on the same page. "Because I'll gut you if you get in my way."

He smiled, but it didn't reach his eyes. "I'm glad we understand each other."

Fabienne snorted. The silence between them grew. Apprehensive with unfinished business. But underneath it was something else—a reluctant alliance. They would work together, because they had to. They would survive, because there was no other option. But when it came to Désakré, there would be no allies. Only opportunity. Risk. Betrayal.

Somewhere beyond the walls, the ethèr lanterns flickered, casting distorted shadows that writhed across the floor like smoke. Finally a Crescent surfaced, gave them marching orders, and left them to their scheming.

Fabienne couldn't tell when she'd fallen asleep, but dawn had come too soon. She woke to a heavy, unnatural silence. Her body ached. Her limbs were sluggish and uncooperative. Her thoughts were slow, hazy. She blinked, adjusting to the low light of the space around her. She was surrounded by stone walls. There was a single archway to the left and a faint wind blew outside.

She was in a different room now—larger than a cell, smaller than a holding chamber. Her wrists were bound with coarse rope, her wings still locked in iron. The cuffs pulsed with faint gilded sigils, biting against the ethèr trying to flow through her. Her pulse thudded dully in her ears.

"Finally awake, pretty little thief?"

Her head snapped toward the voice, her body

reacting before her brain could. She turned and found the Vagabond of Xodom sitting across from her, too comfortable. He had one leg stretched out while the other bent, his arm resting lazily on his knee like he hadn't just been given a death sentence by the Noirmother. His honey-and-amber eyes gleamed in the low light, far too amused.

Fabienne's vision sharpened. She gritted her teeth. "How long have you been sitting there?"

His grin was infuriatingly slow. "Long enough."

A flicker of heat burned under her skin. She hated him. Hated his easy confidence. Hated the way he looked at her like this was a game. She pulled against her restraints, grinding her teeth as the chains dug into her wrists. Her breath slowed. There was a give. A broken link. With a sharp twist and a pull, the chains popped loose.

Havoc let out a low whistle. "Impressive."

Fabienne ignored him. She flexed her fingers once, rolled her shoulders, and turned her attention to her wing restraints. The cuffs bit into her wings, sending shocks of discomfort through her back and down her spine. She gritted her teeth, twisted and snapped. A sharp sting followed, but the weight lifted. Her wings flared out with a groan of stiff joints. She stood slowly, shaking off the remaining fog. Her gaze locked onto the Vagabond—and then froze.

Her eyes dropped to his hand. He held a blade.

And tucked beneath his blade, dangled a key.

Fabienne stared. Her breath caught in her throat.

"You…" Her voice came low, brittle with disbelief. "You had the key to my chains this whole time?"

Havoc grinned wolfishly, spinning the key between his fingers. "I wanted to see how long it would take you to break free."

She lunged at him. He dodged fast—too fast—and she nearly missed slamming into the stone wall.

"You—" She rounded on him, wings flared wide. "Filthy, good for nothing, piece of *rot*."

"Accurate," he said, ducking another swing.

She advanced again, but stopped herself. Killing him now would solve nothing. She exhaled through clenched teeth and turned her back on him, chest rising and falling with fury. She stepped toward the archway and looked out.

The terrain beyond was steep, shadowed by towering, knotted trees that swayed without wind. Purple mist clung low to the ground, curling like tendrils around gnarled roots. The air carried a faint, pulsing hum—like a heartbeat embedded in the soil. She knew where they were.

"The Craven Wood," she whispered.

Havoc rose behind her, brushing dust from his

pants. "At least the Noirmother didn't drop us off on the opposite side of the city."

Fabienne flew out from the safety of the chamber, ignoring him. She wouldn't speak to him. She wouldn't even acknowledge him if she didn't have to.

Fabienne studied the edge of the Craven Wood. She knew all the stories. For one, it was cursed. Down to the very roots that upheld it. Every part of the Wood was malevolent. She'd hid in its outskirts long enough to know its many dangers. Unnatural beasts lived in the Wood. Whispers roamed through the trees. It was said even the stars bent strangely over this place.

Now why would the Noirmother bring them here? To get to Takari, they would need to go through a portal entry. Why would she bring them to the Wood, so far from the nearest portal? The Vagabond floated to her side again, refusing to be ignored.

"We'll have to cross the Wood, survive the Craven, and make it to the river, to get into Taétàn territory."

Fabienne stared at him, partly in annoyance because she hated hearing him talk. Also because she was a bit curious as to how he knew all of that information.

"The river? Why?"

He studied her before answering. "Because the other end of the river will place us in Takari close to the catacombs. It'll be a shorter journey than trying to go through a regular portal."

Fabienne nodded, turning away from him again. Before she could argue further, in the distance there came a rustle.

Fabienne and Emmanuel turned in unison. Movement stirred close to the tree lines.

There was a whistle. Piercing. Familiar.

Fabienne's blood ran cold.

The Ukaveli had found her.

CHAPTER 12

FABIENNE

Fabienne Evruel didn't panic easily. Such emotional reactions were for the weak. She was too methodical, too calculated for such notions. But in this moment, watching the throng of Ukaveli mobsters shoot up from their hidden perches, an uncontrollable kind of fear began flooding her veins.

"Stars! How are the Ukaveli here? How did they find us? Find me?" she cried.

Havoc pulled out his dagger lazily, weighing eyes watching the Ukaveli advance. "They probably got tipped off by the Noirmother. You know, to keep things interesting."

The Ukaveli enforcers broke from the city's edge. Fabienne counted six, no seven, cloaked in shadows and wielding weapons that glowed faintly with summoned ethèr. Their faces were obscured by the hood of their cloaks. At the nape of their cloaks, they donned their Ukaveli sigils with pride. They moved in formation, and with precision, their intent plain. If she and Emmanuel didn't get moving, they'd be dead before the quest even began.

"Fly?" Havoc asked casually.

"Fly!"

Fabienne's wings snapped open with a powerful thrust just as the first arrow zipped past her cheek. She surged upward, Havoc close behind. The trees tore past them in a blur, branches clawing at their arms and legs. Shouts echoed behind them, blades scraping bark, wings tearing through the dawn. Below, the Craven Wood shifted. It moved and breathed. At some point, Fabienne heard when it began to whisper.

"Don't stop," she growled. "Not for anything."

"I'm spontaneous, Reaver. Not stupid," Havoc responded.

They dove through a break in the canopy. The forest swallowed them whole—an endless maze of black trees, glowing spores, and creatures watching from the darkened hollows. Here in the Wood, though it was only the first light of dawn, it looked as if the dusknite had only just begun. The air grew denser, each breath laced with something ancient.

Fabienne felt her nerves fraying. She hated every moment of this, but they had no choice. They had to cross this accursed Wood. As they raced away from the Ukaveli, flying deeper into the Wood, the forest swallowed them whole.

Fabienne flew low, weaving between twisted trunks and tangled branches. The trees here didn't just grow—they loomed. Massive things, knotted and wide like old bones, their bark warped into grotesque ridges and gnarled faces. Some wept sap the color of ink. Others groaned when wind passed through their limbs. The wind liked to whisper songs here. Curses wrapped in sweet melodies to trap you for a lifetime. Unintelligible screams sounded somewhere in the distance to their left.

"The Craven," Fabienne breathed, hardly audible over the beat of her wings.

The forest fed on fear. Terror. Anguish. Just about everything she was currently, wrestling inside as she kept flying. Without trying, she was turning herself into a target, and an offering.

The Wood was an expanse carved from cursed earth and sealed with ancient judgment. Domenents told their young to avoid it. Angels were often banished to it, their judges knowing full well they wouldn't survive long. Now she was flying through the forsaken forest, with a vagabond at her side and death on her heels. Behind them, the sound of pursuit faded.

"Do you hear that?" Havoc called ahead, breathless.

"I'm trying not to," she quipped.

Because she did hear it. Not just the sounds of beasts. Not just the rustle of wings or the flapping of distant movement. Over and over again, she kept hearing her name.

"Fabienne…"

Soft. Distant. Ancient. She whipped her head toward the sound—but there was nothing. Just mist curling around a fallen tree. Stillness so complete it made her breath sound too loud. She beat her wings harder. Her muscles screamed and her body ached. Her face still burned where the Noirmother's Fraetèn had hit her. But she pushed through it. Because failure was unacceptable. She had to survive this quest. She had to find Désakré.

Fabienne thought of Jeduriel as the Shaiths dragged him into the Noirmother's sanctum—at least, what was left of him. She remembered his eyes most of all. The way they still held hope, even when everything else had been stripped away. How they had, for a moment, flickered with defiance. Then she thought of how the Crescent had siphoned Jeduriel's fôrs, and given him a permanent, angelic death.

Fabienne swallowed hard, bile rising in her throat. She wasn't ready to die. She wasn't ready to be gone from Tatiana.

An image came unbidden. Her sisari's smile. Tatiana's laughter when Fabienne taught her to fly for the first time. She had been small, frail almost, but full of life and curiosity. She'd been nervous, but she'd finally spread her wings, and flown just a few feet off the rooftops before settling back down. Tatiana had been so proud, and Fabienne had hugged her and laughed, encouraging her to try again, but longer this time.

Fabienne clenched her fists mid-flight, her nails digging into her palms. She couldn't afford to fail. She couldn't afford to trust. Not the Fraetèn. Not the Wood. And definitely not *him*.

She glanced sideways at Havoc. His wings beat effortlessly, even after everything. His gaze scanned the forest with a cool shrewedness that unsettled her. She still didn't understand him. What was in all of this for him? And why was he the Vagabond of Xodom anyway? What was his story? His purpose?

She thought of earlier, while she was still in shackles. He'd had a key. He'd watched her struggle. And he'd smiled through it all like this was just another game to win.

She hated him for it.

But she needed him. For now.

"Do you know the way?" she asked without preamble.

Havoc nodded, eyes fixed ahead. "I know enough."

"That's not an answer."

"It's the only one you're getting until we make it to the river."

Fabienne bit back a curse.

Around them, the trees thickened. The mist grew denser. And still the Wood offered no warmth, no welcome. Only dread. They flew in silence for a while longer, until even the sound of their wings seemed too loud. Fabienne felt it in her chest first—a pressure, like the air was thickening around them. Ethèr buzzed unnaturally across her skin, like she'd flown through an invisible veil. She slowed.

Havoc noticed and hovered just behind her. "What is it?"

She didn't speak. Just drifted lower, her senses stretching into the terrain. The ground below was cracked and pale, like bone. The trees didn't grow here—they leaned, twisted toward some unseen source deeper in the woods. Even the wind had gone still.

Then she saw them.

Etchings.

Dozens of them, carved into the trunks of a circular grove—spirals, symbols, sigils in languages no one had spoken in a thousand cycles. Some glowed faintly. Others wept black resin. This was a warning to outsiders. Get lost or suffer the consequences.

"We shouldn't be here," she murmured.

A snort. "Too late now," Havoc answered.

She turned to him. There was no smugness in his face. Only seriousness. Maybe even fear. And somehow, that unsettled her more than anything else. She opened her mouth to speak—but stopped. Because something in the forest had changed. Not a sound, nor movement. But a feeling. Like the forest had turned to look at them.

The Craven Wood knew they were here. And it was very curious.

Fabienne's hearts skipped several beats.

"We need to keep moving," she said quickly.

Havoc didn't argue. They launched back into the air, higher this time, weaving through the tangled canopy as a mist rose, swallowing the grove behind them. Fabienne didn't look back.

But she felt it.

The Wood wasn't chasing them.

It was watching. And it was waiting.

CHAPTER 13

EMMANUEL

Emmanuel Alfonse flew through the canopy of the Craven Wood, cursing himself for the thousandth time for not listening to Yolanda's warning. Had he taken her seriously, he could be anywhere else right now minding his business. He'd always been good at sneaking out of situations like this. Or fighting his way out if he had to. Now, he was trapped.

The air of the Wood continued to cluster as he pressed further into the forest. He noticed there was also a pressure—the kind that sank into his wings and lungs, heavy and suffocating. Everything here whispered with an edge. The trees looked twisted by time and sorrow, their limbs clawing at the sky like they were trying to pull it down. He imagined there must have been a time, long ago, when the Craven Wood was something entirely different. He mused for some time on what could've turned the forest into this mesh of deaden trees and monstrous creatures. Not that he really cared. But he always did love a good story.

A low hum pulsed through the soil, hardly detectable. Emmanuel felt it crawl under his skin like a thousand invisible needles. It wasn't just the weight of mist or the unnatural silence that stretched between the twisted branches—it was a presence. Ancient. Still breathing. It clung to his senses, sinking into the fabric of his leathers, even his wings, making them heavier, slower. This place was haunted and he wanted to get the hèls out.

Get in the catacombs. Get Désakré. Get out...without the thief.

That was the plan. He just had to ditch the irritatingly beautiful Reaver and he could be on his way.

Emmanuel angled his wings and picked up speed, glancing back once to make sure she was following. She was. Of course she was. Her precision was a growing annoyance. She flew like she was carved from wind and fire, every motion angular and deliberate. Always on his heels, always questioning.

"Do you feel that?" Her voice was quieter now, carrying over the wind.

Emmanuel's jaw tightened. Of course he felt it. The weight pressing down on them was more than the chill of the Wood—it was a pulse. A rhythm vibrating beneath the surface. Like a heartbeat. But admitting that would only give her an excuse to challenge him more.

"You know where you're going?"

This wasn't the first time she asked this. Her constant questioning was starting to grate on his nerves.

Emmanuel rolled his eyes. "Would it matter if I didn't?"

"Considering I don't want to die in here? Yes."

He let out a long, mocking sigh. "How tragic, dearest Reaver. Guess we better keep flying, then."

Her wings flared slightly as she surged forward. He could feel her frowning even if he didn't look. He smiled at himself. If she was going to get on his nerves, two could play that game.

He dipped lower through a break in the canopy, eyes scanning the terrain. The forest floor below shimmered with faint, bioluminescent moss. The trees glowed in pulses like veins. His mind drifted—back to the legends whispered about the Craven Wood. Tales of Domenents who wandered too deep, their ethèr consumed by unseen hands, leaving only husks behind. He'd never put much stock in ghost stories. Now? He'd wished he'd listened. A fleeting memory of his pasari crossed his mind. He remembered being small and innocent. Remembered his papa sitting him on the knee, and filling his imagination with endless stories that left him in wonder. Then the Fallen came.

Emmanuel scowled. He immediately crushed the thought. Every memory of his father was too painful to bear. Reaver's voice cut through his mangled thoughts.

"Havoc."

He flinched at the use of his street name. He didn't know why he wished she'd use his real name instead.

Idiot. She's not your friend. Focus.

"You're quieter than usual. Not planning to betray me already, are you?"

"Not yet, my conniving Void Reaver," he purred.

A flicker of amusement flittered across her face. "Good. I'd hate to kill you before we find Désakré."

Emmanuel snorted. "That's assuming you get to the stone first, pretty little thief."

"Please. You're so confident it won't be me. But I have more to lose. The stakes are greater for me. I will get that stone."

She had more to lose? How did she know that? If only she knew what was really after him. If she knew why he was always on the run, why he could never stay in one place too long... If she knew why he was called a Vagabond, she'd eat her words.

But Emmanuel didn't correct her. He chose to stay silent.

The weight of unseen eyes dragged on his shoulders. The Craven Wood was more than cursed. It was hungry. He felt it pulse. A rhythm that echoed at the core of his six beating hearts.

"This place doesn't like us," Reaver murmured, her tone quieter now.

"You think?"

The pulse grew louder. Then there was a flicker of movement between the branches to their left. His instincts screamed to fly away, and fast. He jerked back midair as a blur of fur and fangs launched upward.

"Havoc! What in the rotting skies was—"

A snarl split the silence. Claws slashed towards Emmanuel's face. He twisted, avoiding the strike—

Only to catch a second blow across his shoulder. Agony flared deep, and anguish sang through his bones.

"*Rot!*" He swore, his wings angled wrong, tipping him off-balance. He'd managed to get a glimpse of the creature before it barreled into him.

It was an ogarou.

Another ogarou surfaced, preparing to lunge at

him. Then Reaver was there. She crashed into the creature from the side, pushing Emmanuel clear. Her wings flared wide to slow them both as she spun midair, dagger already in hand. Emmanuel landed hard on a thick branch, rolled, and sprang back into the air. Reaver's blade gleamed as she drove it into the beast's side with a clean, vicious swipe. The ogarou let out a guttural cry and tumbled back.

Reaver turned mid-hover, her eyes blazing. "Distracted much?"

Emmanuel gritted his teeth. "Maybe if you hadn't been talking so much, I would've caught him faster."

"Oh, piss off."

His mouth opened in rebuttal, when more shifty movement swayed in the thick, empty branches. Suddenly, winged mounts burst from the dark, their riders crouched low, weapons drawn.

"No, burning way," Emmanuel cursed.

Reaver seemed frozen. She stared at the beasts, her eyes wide with terror.

"Elledelle to Reaver. Snap out of it!" Emmanuel barked. "The ogarou are riding on battox. *Move* or the battox will have your head!"

Emmanuel's eyes locked onto the strange curved blades in the hands of the ogarou—long, jagged things humming with majik—cursed ethèr first brought into existence from the Fallen.

"Go for their heads," Emmanuel cried.

Without answering, Reaver threw herself into the malay, doing exactly as he said.

The first ogarou dove, and the fight erupted.

Emmanuel surged forward to meet the attack. His blade clashed against the ogarou's, the shockwave of their majik against his ethèr colliding in a burst of shadow and light. He twisted, kicked the ogarou square in the chest, and slashed across—a clean, cutting arc through its neck that sent obsidian blood spattering.

Reaver was in her own dance of blood and survival. Her wings cut through the air in tight sweeps as she flipped backward, dodging two ogarou and driving her heel into the jaw of a third. Her dagger sang as it danced in her hand.

Emmanuel spun through the chaos, ethèr sparking at his fingertips. With a snap of his wrist, he sent a shockwave outward—a concussive blast that threw one ogarou off their battox. A little ways from him, Reaver wove through three battox without riders like water, her wings skimming their leathery hides, her blades drawing swift, fatal cuts.

Emmanuel's mind enlightened. This attack wasn't random. The monsters weren't just here to stop them. They were trying to guard something. But what?

The last ogarou fell, screaming into the fog. The woods grew quiet again, as if exhaling.

Emmanuel and Fabienne hovered in place, catching their breath. Emmanuel's shoulder ached, but his mind buzzed. Reaver was a thorn. She was infuriating. But stars, she could fight.

He adjusted his grip on his blade, looking at her one more time. The air in the distance across the clearing pulsed. Both their heads snapped forward. Then they saw it.

An ethereal barrier splitting the Wood.

CHAPTER 14

EMMANUEL

Emmanuel and Fabienne ogled the mythical barrier, completely blindsided by its presence. They were so entangled with the ogarou and battox, they hadn't even realized the ethereal divide was there.

"What in stars is that?" Emmanuel exclaimed, his eyes widening at the sight before him.

He blinked at the shimmering wall, unsure of what to make of it. It wasn't just a barrier. It seemed more like a seal of sorts. The wall spanned the length of the Wood's inner border, glittering like glass infused with stormlight. Emmanuel couldn't tell where the wall ended, and where it began again. It was breathtaking in beauty, and clearly was born of an otherworldly power. But still. Something about it felt *wrong*.

Etched along its surface were faint, twinkling symbols. Emmanuel lifted a hand, as if to touch them, but Reaver swatted his hand away. He spun on her, ready to tell her off, but her eyes were glued to the words. She hovered beside him, her expression grim. Her gaze was locked on the symbols, her wings beating slower, as if instinct warned her to retreat.

"I've… read about these." Her voice was quieter now, almost reverent. "This is an Etherien Seal."

Emmanuel's brows knit together. "A what?"

Reaver's jaw tightened, her gaze never leaving the wall. "It's a Seal, Havoc. Made by an Etherien. You know, angels like us who actually don't live entirely crappy lives? They had to have been a Judge, too. Or even an Establisher, perhaps. This isn't a barrier. This is a prison."

Emmanuel's gut twisted. A prison? For what? Better yet, for *whom*?

He didn't ask because he wasn't sure he wanted the answer.

"They used Domènn to write this," he murmured, noticing some of the familiar words in the native language of Domenents. "But it doesn't seem like it's from our Age."

He recognized the faint glow of ancient glyphs, though he couldn't decipher them. The symbols danced along the barrier's surface, moving with an energy that whispered of chains and oblivion.

"These are from the First Age," Reaver whispered, her voice strained. "At the initial creation of our Elstar, Gamarh. There weren't any kingdoms back then, and only the one language. Plus, only Domenents lived here. Before the Fallen began to arrive."

"And it's still holding?" Emmanuel's voice was skeptical, but even as he spoke, he felt the pull in his ethèr—a magnetic force warning him not to go any closer.

"Hardly. It's been here a long time, and it's definitely been tampered with."

Reaver's wings beat a little slower now, her eyes narrowing as she drifted closer, studying the barrier. Her expression darkened, a flicker of something almost… haunted.

"This isn't meant to keep us out, Havoc." Her eyes flickered to him, a small flash of fear coloring her multicolored pale irises with darkness. "This was meant to keep something, or someone, in."

Emmanuel's throat went dry.

"Well, whatever it is, it's still locked away." He forced a smirk, masking the unease crawling up his spine. "We just need to get past it."

Reaver didn't respond, her gaze fixed on the impossible wall before them.

"And how in the burning stars are we supposed to do that," she quipped, eyes still glued to the wall. "To get past it, we have to go through it. If we break it, we might let out whatever has been trapped inside for eons."

Emmanuel felt his patience with this quest thinning. Why in all the realms would the Fraetèn send them this way knowing it would be impossible? The way forward had just gotten a lot more complicated than he expected. They couldn't go back, and they couldn't go around. But they also couldn't go through. So what on this Elstar were they supposed to do?

The barrier pulsed again, but this time, Emmanuel swore he heard something.

A whisper through his mind.

Emmanuel Litheriel Alfonse, the Brave. We will collect our debt, Vagabond. You still belong to us.

It slithered through his mind, curling like smoke around his thoughts, faint but undeniable. Emmanuel floated, frozen in place. The voice was dark and familiar while belonging to many though they sounded like one. His ethèr stirred, reacting to whatever ancient force hummed beneath the surface of that shimmering wall. He felt it in his bones. In his blood.

"Havoc?"

He blinked, realizing he'd been staring at the barrier too long. His wings had unconsciously stopped beating, his body hovering midair as if something had taken hold of him.

"You okay?" Reaver's gaze cut through him, sifting for the truth, her expression tight with the concern she was trying to hide.

"Fine," he lied, forcing his wings to beat again, pushing the strange sensation away. The last thing he needed was Reaver asking questions he didn't have answers to. "Just thinking."

Her eyes narrowed, but she didn't press. Thank the stars. He wasn't ready to explain what he'd felt—or heard.

"We need to get through it." Emmanuel gestured toward the barrier. "You know how these work, right? Etherien Seals?"

Reaver hovered closer, her eyes fixed on the glowing symbols. Her expression was unreadable, but he could tell the gears of her mind were hard at work. "I know enough to know we shouldn't be near one."

"That's not helpful."

"It's the truth." Her tone was clipped, her jaw locked.

That was her tell.

She was worried.

"Can you break it?" Emmanuel asked, his voice lower now, almost hopeful. They had to get past this stars-forsaken barrier. Especially before anymore ogarou came back.

Reaver didn't answer immediately.

"I don't know." She looked askance at him. "This is ancient ethèr. I don't... I don't think I have what it takes to break this. We may need to find a way around—"

"There is no way around," Emmanuel cut her off. "We go through or we're dead. Those are our options. Don't think the Noirmother won't make her way in here to find out if we did the job or not. And if she comes, the Ukaveli will, too. We need to get through this thing."

Reaver didn't answer. She didn't have to. The tension in her posture was loud enough.

"We're wasting time," Emmanuel growled, impatience burning in his veins. He couldn't afford to hesitate. Every moment they lingered put them behind. He drew his dagger, the edge catching the faint glow of the barrier's light. "We go through."

"Havoc, wait—"

Too late. He pressed the tip of his blade against the shimmering surface. The reaction was immediate.

A shockwave of ethèr rippled outward, slammed into Emmanuel's chest and sent him flying backward. His wings flared instinctively, steadying him before he crashed into the twisted branches behind him.

"Burning idiot!" Reaver hissed, her wings snapping as she shot toward him.

Emmanuel groaned, pain lancing through his chest where the blast had struck. "I had to try."

"No, you didn't." Reaver's glare could've melted steel. Her hands hovered just over his chest, where the ethèr had left faint scorch marks. "Do you ever think before you act?"

"Not if I can help it." He tried to smirk, but it came out as more of a grimace. "What just happened?"

Reaver's mouth worked, screwing into a scowl. "The Seal stopped you." She glanced back toward the barrier, her eyes narrowing. "Whatever's behind that wall… it doesn't want you near it."

"Great. Love that for me."

"This isn't a joke, Havoc." Her voice was harder now, her frustration breaking through the cracks in her usually measured exterior. "If you had touched it with your ethèr, it could have shattered you from the inside out."

Emmanuel stiffened, eyes gingerly dancing back to the wall.

“Any other options?”

Reaver's brows furrowed. “I'm still thinking it through—”

“Oh for rotting sake.” Emmanuel pushed to sit up and the world spun once. Twice.

"Just give me a moment! Burning stars," she hissed. "Take a breather. You need it anyway. Give me a chance to think back on what I know and if it can help us get through."

Emmanuel didn't want to wait. But the pain spreading through his entire body made him slow down enough to realize she was right.

"Fine."

"Fine."

Reaver, satisfied he wouldn't try anything stupid, floated away. He felt a pang of cold at her absence from his side. And in the quiet, the voices returned.

We will collect our debt, Vagabond. You still belong to us.

CHAPTER 15

FABIENNE

When Fabienne was a youngling, no more than six or seven, she'd loved hearing old tales whispered in the quiet before the evening fire. Xodom would get chilly dusks, and her masari would make her and Tatiana hot tea that made her insides warm like the sumyrin season.

Fabienne would tuck herself away into the corner of their comfy cloudcouch and dive into the scrolls about Etheriens of old. Etheriens were angels, of differing rank, who were all holy and loyal to Ehyeh in some way. It didn't mean they were perfect, or didn't have their faith in the Sovereign tested, but even in their worst state, they hadn't been abased enough to become Fallen.

Much like herself. She was a thief with a life full

of grievous sins, but to Ehyeh, she was still an Etherien. She hadn't reached the place where she'd be made into being a Fallen. Yet. Fabienne thought she would never be able to understand such grace.

Many Etheriens, throughout the Ages were commissioned by Ehyeh with a specific purpose. Some were chosen. Others simply rose to meet the occasion and were memorialized throughout history. Some of those Etheriens had the ability to create powerful things her small mind couldn't understand at the time. Things like Etherien Seals.

Fabienne hovered midair, staring at the barrier. She remembered reading about how they were done. She couldn't bring to mind every detail and that annoyed her, because now she needed to remember it all. But she did recall one part of the scroll mentioning these seals had been infused with the ethèr of the angel who made it.

And something else.

But what?

Try as she might, she just couldn't remember what else they did to create the Seal and keep it there for eons. It pulsed now with that glimmering, iridescent glow.

Defeat curled at the edges of her resolve, threatening to sink into her bones, but she forced it down. She couldn't give up. Désakré was on the other side. Tatiana's life was on the other side. Paying off her debt to the Ukaveli was on the other side. She had to get to Désakré—before Havoc did.

Fabienne turned toward a clearing a few meters away, avoiding the Pandemir. If he stretched his ethèr, his brutish strength would be maximized to cataclysmic proportions. He really would be able to break through the wall. But at what cost? She still needed him to get to the catacombs. If he died trying to punch through the Seal, in the end it wouldn't solve anything.

She floated away, frowning at the sinking sôl above. The Craven Wood was quickly getting darker, and that made her uncomfortable. The ground was uneven but solid enough to make camp for the dusknite.

She landed lightly, her boots pressing into the soft earth as she scanned the area. Havoc hovered above, watching. Probably waiting for her to do all the work.

Fabienne rolled her shoulders, sighing deep. "I'll set us up here. You—" She glanced up at him. "Can find food. Water."

Havoc smirked. "Desperate to be alone with the Etherien Seal, are we?"

Fabienne didn't humor him with a response. She simply arched a brow.

Havoc sighed dramatically. "Fine, fine. But if I

don't come back, you're on your own with the ogarou and battox." He paused, grinning wider. "Oh, and the Fraetèn and Ukaveli."

Shaking with laughter, he flew away.

Fabienne scoffed. "By the stars. How did I end up here? And with *him* no less?"

His laugh was the last thing she heard before he flew off into the darkened wood hunting for whatever they could scrap into a meal.

Alone, Fabienne focused on making their temporary camp. She moved with practiced ease, gathering what little kindling she could find. The Craven Wood was strange—too silent, too still. There were no birds, or squirrels. No pockets of flowers could be found alive here. The Wood looked dead, though it was anything but that. She knew it was alive and would devour everything it could. Still, it was silent, dark, empty, and filled with a dread that weighed down her spirit. It set her nerves on edge, but she ignored the feeling and worked fast. The fire crackled to life easily enough, casting flickering shadows across the trees. It wasn't much, but it would hold.

She took a seat, stretching her sore limbs. Every inch of her body ached. In less than two dawns, shed been captured, beaten, stolen from, threatened, fought with unnatural woodland monsters, and been thrown into an impossible mission. She was filthy, hungry, and exhausted. She glanced at her fingernails and looked away. She looked as unkempt as she felt. Her leathers still had dried blood on them, and her locs felt heavy with sweat, blood, and tangles. She exhaled slowly, willing herself to focus.

The job wasn't hygiene. The job was to get the stone and get out... before Havoc or the Fraetèn triple crossed her. She had to think ahead. Solve this current problem. Keep moving, then get out of this suicide quest.

She reached into the satchel still strapped at her side. It clung to her since she'd been dumped with the Vagabond at Xodom's city edge. The Fraetèn saw fit to give it back, with all the contents inside, plus some more to help her fend for herself until she made it to the catacombs in Takari. Thank the stars for that small mercy. Her fingers brushed over a small piece of jewelry folded tightly within. She pulled it out, unfolding the chain just enough to reveal the faint twinkle of golden etchings and design.

It was Tatiana's locket. She'd given it to Fabienne as a keepsake long before she'd gotten entangled with the traitorous Taétàn. Each time Fabienne thought of the giants, she wanted to spit fire. The two sisters had each gotten lockets made many cycles ago, then given them to each other as gifts. Now it was the painful memory of a time long passed that Fabienne was desperate to reclaim.

Fabienne clenched her jaw, pushing down the ache in her chest. She didn't allow herself to linger, instead tucking it back into the satchel and focusing on the fire. She would finish this job and free herself, and her sisari, once and for all.

CHAPTER 16

FABIENNE

Fabienne's eyes flickered up from the ivory and scarlet of the fire, snagging onto Havoc's easy gait into the clearing. She'd nearly convinced herself he had actually gotten himself killed since he'd taken so long. Havoc came to land with an effortless grace, tossing something onto the ground between them. A small bundle wrapped in leaves.

"Supprèst."

Fabienne lifted a brow. "Is my dinner poisoned?"

"No promises." He smirked before pulling out a flask of water and handing it to her. "I figure you'd rather dehydrate than trust me, but here."

She took it without comment, uncorking it and taking a slow sip. The water was clean, fresh, and soothing. Her eyes fluttered shut as she enjoyed the moment. Then she sighed, opening them again. Stars. She felt heavy. So heavy. Weighed down by her burdens and woes. Would she always live like this? In the shadows, or on the fly? From one syndicate to the next? Would she never know true freedom?

Havoc watched her with an unreadable expression, and frankly, she was too tired to care. Fabienne pulled the food bundle open, and without thinking twice, bit down and began eating. Havoc joined her, and they ate in relative silence, the fire flickering between them. The tension that usually lingered in the air had softened just slightly, dulled by extreme fatigue and wariness.

After a while, Havoc leaned back, stretching out his wings. "So," he said, "Désakré."

Fabienne almost groaned out loud. For once, she didn't want to talk about it. She was so. Burning. *Tired*. "What about it, Havoc?"

He eyed her carefully. "Why do you want it?"

She considered him a moment before answering.

"It's a solution to several of my problems."

Havoc's gaze lingered on her. "So, this isn't just a job for you."

Fabienne's fingers tightened around the flask. No. It wasn't.

Havoc didn't press. Instead, he turned his focus to

the barrier. “I was thinking,” he said, voice lighter, “what are the chances the prison isn't empty?”

Fabienne glanced at him sharply.

“You don't think...”

“Oh. But, I do.”

A cold sensation ran through her spine. She followed his gaze. Her stomach turned.

“You believe there are Faedes in there?”

Havoc tapped his fingers against his knee. “Correct.”

Fabienne inhaled through her nose, steadying her nerves. Faedes were the Fallen equivalent of Domenents and utterly horrifying. She never, in all her existence, ever wanted to face one. Especially not head on or alone.

“But we have to break the Seal to cross.”

“Exactly.”

"Which means we'd be letting them out..."

Havoc’s smirk faltered, just slightly. But his eyes were empty of their usual mirth. “Bingo.”

Silence stretched between them.

“Few things in this Elstar terrify me like Faedes do.”

Havoc stilled, saying nothing. His expression had shifted—one that concerned Fabienne, though she said nothing aloud. The fire crackled between them.

The dusknite pressed in closer, shadows stretching long against the trees.

Fabienne's eyes stayed locked on the barrier. Even from this distance, it pulsed with that eerie, almost sentient glow. Every instinct in her body screamed to get away from it. To turn back. To leave whatever waited beyond untouched.

But she couldn't.

"Fabienne."

Havoc's voice pulled her out of her thoughts. The sound of her name, not Reaver, but her true name, toyed at something sensitive in her chest that shook and shimmied, trying to wedge its way out. She swallowed around a lump, crushing the feeling. She blinked, realizing she'd been staring at the barrier for a long while. Too long. The firelight danced across his face as he watched her—his usual smirk absent, replaced by something unreadable.

"You're thinking pretty loud." His tone was soft. Less mocking.

"Wasn't on purpose. Promise." She murmured, her throat thick for some odd reason. What was this *thing* she was feeling? And why was she feeling it now?

"Want to process it out loud?"

No. Stars, no.

She glanced at him, his amber-and-honey eyes reflecting the flicker of the flames. All of his normal sarcasm and arrogance were gone. To her, this was more dangerous than any of his blades. She wanted his cockiness, not his vulnerability. Because if he lowered his barriers, she'd have to lower hers, too. And that would be her undoing.

"Why do you care?" She asked, willing a cold, biting, sharpness into her voice.

Havoc didn't flinch. His expression stayed the same. He leaned forward, the full weight of his attention on her.

"I'm not stupid, Fabienne." His voice was calm. So calm. And unexpectedly caring. And he'd said Fabienne, not Reaver. He'd said her name, again. Stars, what was happening?

"You said you had far more to lose. Higher stakes in this than me. This is all weighing on you... differently. Talking it out can help."

Fabienne's jaw clenched. He wasn't wrong.

"I told you, it's a solution." She tried to keep her voice neutral, but the ache in her chest made it impossible.

"You're too intelligent to be a common thief. That's more than obvious. The stone is more than just a *solution*." Havoc's gaze didn't waver. "You're not trying to fix something. You're trying not to *lose* it."

Fabienne's stomach twisted. He was too close to the truth. She opted to keep her mouth shut. She turned back toward the fire, willing him to disappear. But she could still feel his eyes on her—like he could see straight through her.

"What's wrong?"

"It's nothing," she said, forcing her voice to steady.

"Liar."

Fabienne's wings twitched, her grip tightening around the flask she hadn't realized she was still holding.

"Don't push me, Emmanuel," she murmured, her tone carrying a warning. His name slipped out of her mouth, unbidden. And that *thing* in her chest, continued unraveling. To her surprise, he didn't press. He only gave a small smile and let the silence between them stretch.

"Fine," he said after a long moment, leaning back again with his usual ease and carelessness. He stretched his wings before shaking out his short, auburn locs. "Keep your secrets, my pretty little thief."

CHAPTER 17

EMMANUEL

The eerie quiet of the Craven Wood was an unsettling, tangible thing that made Emmanuel's insides quiver. He was beginning to feel the longer they were in the wood, the slower time was moving. It felt like a trap for a slow fade into unending oblivion. This was their first dusk here, and it felt like their seventh.

The fire crackled, its glow flickering against the rough bark of the surrounding trees. The unnatural hush of the Craven Wood pressed in on them, but neither Emmanuel nor Fabienne moved to break it. Not yet.

Fabienne had spoken of the Faedes. From what she'd said, she hadn't encountered any, but she knew enough about them to be terrified. Her voice had been tight. Her fingers had curled against her knee. She was afraid and had every reason to be.

He hadn't interrupted her. For the first time in a long time, he didn't want to be sarcastic. Not in that kind of moment. Emmanuel watched Fabienne close up, demanding to be left with her secrets. But yet, he found his own screaming to be let out.

Emmanuel gave himself the rare luxury of tumbling deep into his thoughts. Something within his chest burned. A feeling he couldn't quite put into words. It had been with him since he'd come of age, and it had never let him go. It always surfaced at the mention of the Fallen. The Faedes. The ones who took without remorse. The ones who had taken from him until he had nothing left in all the realms.

Emmanuel could feel Fabienne watching him carefully now, tilting her head.

"You're angry."

Emmanuel let out a slow breath, rolling his jaw. "A little."

"Have you dealt with a Faede before, Emmanuel?"

Emmanuel exhaled sharply, leaning forward, resting his elbows on his knees. He let his gaze settle on the fire. He stayed quiet, a long time, before deciding to fess up. Chances are, before this quest was done, he might be dead. May as well fess up now to this stranger and get some parts of his true story off of his chest.

"I was seven," he said finally. His voice felt foreign, heavy. "That's when they came for me."

Fabienne went still.

"Pasari... he always knew they would," Emmanuel continued. "Faedes don't forget a blood debt. My family… my bloodline… someone had made a bargain, ages before us. A bargain that cost every generation since. My basari's—" His throat tightened. He forced himself to keep his voice even. "I didn't know I had brothers. I was the youngest. Every single one of them had been taken before I was born."

The fire popped, a spark flaring up before dying into embers.

"Pasari tried to stop it," he went on. "Tried to keep me hidden. I don't remember much, just… the dusk everything changed. I remember the shadows shifting, the sky breaking open. The sound of wings—not like ours. He told me to fly, but I didn't. I saw him fight them." Emmanuel clenched his fists. "And I saw him fail. And fall."

Fabienne was silent for a long time. Then, softly, "How did you escape?"

Emmanuel's lips curved, but there was no humor in it. "I didn't. They claimed me."

Fabienne stiffened, but he shook his head. "I got out. I don't know how. I was young. But something happened. One second, I was bound. The next, everything was burning. The Faedes were gone. I flew, and I never looked back."

Silence filled the clearing. The weight of his words settled into the air between the fire's glow and the deep shadows beyond it.

Fabienne's gaze lowered, her fingers curling against her lap. "Your pasari…"

"Father died fighting," Emmanuel finished. His voice was steady, but the edge beneath it was impossible to miss. "And I've been running ever since." He grinned, but there was no joy in it. "Xodom's infamous, Vagabond."

Fabienne's eyes shadowed as she let out a slow breath, staring into the flames. She looked despondent and grieved.

"We're both thieves," Fabienne muttered. "But we were stolen from first."

Something about the way she said it made Emmanuel's chest constrict. He glanced at her, and for the first time, he saw past her calculated control. Saw past the cold fire of her determination and the carefully built walls around her. He saw an aèl who had lost just as much as he had.

Emmanuel studied Fabienne as she turned to him

and met his gaze. He looked into her eyes, both pale, one light light and the other like liquid silver. He wouldn't admit it out loud, but she was so strikingly beautiful. And her eyes, they were older than her, bearing a weight he knew was mirrored in his own. Without a word, they somehow came to an understanding. They weren't allies. But at least they understood each other.

The fire began dying. The embers glowed softly, their light casting a dull orange sheen against the shadows stretching beyond the clearing. Neither of them made to sleep, even though dawn would be upon them soon. Emmanuel watched the fading flames, his mind on the last legs of this quest.

Cross the river, enter the catacombs, steal the stone from the King of giants' grave.

He knew neither him nor Fabienne had any intention of leaving this mission empty-handed.

The air between them grew heavier, somber with the unspoken. Emmanuel was no fool. A moment of borrowed peace wasn't enough to cause either of them to change their intentions. He wanted the stone, and so did she. In the end, it would come down to whoever got it first, and how the other would survive the loss.

"The both of us aren't getting out of this. Not alive. Are we?"

Emmanuel's voice was soft but he wasn't asking a question.

Fabienne's mouth twisted. She didn't answer. Because she didn't have to.

They both knew the truth.

"It doesn't have to be that way," Emmanuel breathed.

Fabienne's eyes rose to meet his.

"Yes, it does," she said quietly, but resolute.

Emmanuel sighed, pulling into himself, his barriers flaring back up, cementing themselves in place.

"Then so be it." He looked away from her. "May the best thief survive."

After a long while, Emmanuel spoke up again.

"The Noirmother showed me a map before we left while you were still asleep." He looked to the barrier, mind far away. "It's a straight shot to the river once we figure out breaking through this thing," he said, jutting his chin at the Etherien Seal.

Fabienne nodded, but remained silent.

"Once we cross the river, we enter Takari, and the Taétàn moonrings." Emmanuel looked to the stars. "Then..." A pause. "Then we head for the catacombs, and into the grave of the Taétàn King."

CHAPTER 18

FABIENNE

The first light of a downcast dawn began to cascade over the length of the clearing into the Craven Wood. Fabienne Evruel had managed a short, fitful rest where she had nightmares about marrying a Taétàn, and being shackled to a Faede through a blood oath, for the rest of her waking existence.

She sat now by the deadened logs of the old fire, frustrated she'd fallen asleep. Waking up like this was probably worse than simply staying up the entire dusknite. She frowned, already weighed down by the rest of the quest. She kept casting a glance at the Etherien Seal, thinking over and over again on what she could do to get through it.

The best idea she could come up with was having Emmanuel draw heavily on his ethèr as a Pandemir and breaking through. But that could burn him out to a husk of himself which meant it wasn't an option. Deep down inside, she had a knowing. Getting through the Etherien Seal would be on her. She'd need to use her ethèr as a Void Reaver. Sift through the Seal's weak points, weaken them further, then break them, until the barrier could no longer hold.

Behind her, she heard Emmanuel stirring. He, too, had an uneasy sleep. He muttered angrily beneath his breath, fighting his enemies in his dreamscape. She'd stopped watching him. She wouldn't allow herself to get attached to the Vagabond.

No. Not Vagabond.

Just *Emmanuel*—an aèn who'd been robbed of everything he loved by the Fallen, and was made to be the Vagabond of Xodom. Her hearts tugged at her as she remembered his story, but she quickly shook it out of her mind. They were not friends. They weren't even allies. But she wouldn't dishonor him any longer by thinking of him as a Vagabond.

The rustle of his wings, his deep and low thrumming sigh, and then his voice, all rose up behind her—still heavy with sleep but laced with mischief. The sound made a few of her wings shiver. She ignored that, too.

"Let's just break through it," he said, his voice low and husky, dripping with slumber.

"Good dawn to you, too, Emmanuel."

He chuckled, yawned deeply, and floated closer to her. She caught a whiff of his scent. Masculine, woodsy, a touch of pine, with hints of aging blood and sweat. Again, her wings rustled, but she squashed the nonsense fluttering in her chest.

"Hear me out. I want to just head on plow through it."

Fabienne sighed, rubbing her temples. "I can't believe you're actually serious about that."

He stretched, rolling his shoulders before cracking his neck. His eyes gleamed with challenge. He squatted down close to her. A little too close. His knees brushed hers, but he didn't make to pull away, and neither did she. She felt jittery at his nearness. It was a feat avoiding looking at him straight in the eyes.

"Dead serious. We've wasted too much time. I say we force our way through."

"First off, we've only been here one entire dusk. The Noirmother gave us twelve dawns. We have a full wèk."

Emmanuel's grin stretched wide, turned wolfish, and became entirely disarming.

"How cute of you to think she meant we could use up all of that time." He leaned forward, one of his wings brushing one of hers. Fabienne barely contained a small yelp at the touch. Something in her burned, and it was all she could do to keep still.

"You want to know what I think is really going on here?"

He didn't wait for her to respond.

"I would bet half my earnings—" Fabienne snorted at that. A thief having earnings was like a grave holding a living body. "That the Noirmother didn't only put *us* up to this," he continued, as if she'd never interrupted him. "I bet you she kidnapped *multiples* of us. Thieves. Vagabonds. Ruffians. All of us in debt to one syndicate or another. And she gave us all the same instructions, and sent us to fetch the same prize."

Fabienne's eyes widened as Emmanuel spoke. The more he talked, the more sense he made, and the more her hatred for the Noirmother grew.

"If we're all after the same prize..." she began.

"First one to get it wins," Emmanuel finished her thought.

"And whoever fails..."

"Dies."

They looked at each other a long, heated moment. Then Fabienne was on her feet floating towards the Etherien Seal. Sudden motivation to break past the Seal and get to those catacombs flooded her bloodstream.

"Don't think me a fool, but I'm going to try something. Just hush, and float over there." She pointed at a little ways off.

For once, Emmanuel obeyed, floating back with a lazy shrug. "What in the stars are you planning, my pretty little thief?"

When had him calling her that started making her feel heady and flushed all at once? Fabienne shook her head clear.

Focus, fool.

"Just hush... and wait."

Fabienne took a slow breath, and floated nearer still to the Etherien Seal. The air around it vibrated, humming against her skin. She could almost hear a whisper at the back of her mind, a beckoning—or a warning. She reached deep, pulling on her Void Reaver ethèr—that sacred power woven into her very being. It gathered at her fingertips, pale light crackling faintly. Then she placed her palms against the Etherien Seal.

Nothing happened.

Her brows furrowed. She felt the resistance, the refusal. Like a being from a previous time rising up to vehemently tell her *no*. But they had to get through. And the only way was to break this damned Seal. Whatever was being imprisoned inside could rot in the lowest levels of the Hèls. She had to get her and Emmanuel passed this barrier.

Fabienne took a deep breath and collected her thoughts. She dug deeper, going so far into her fôrs—her angelic spirit and energy—she could've lost herself. She dove into the very depths of her ethèr, the well of power full, thrumming, and alive inside of her. She began pulling on it, drawing a vast flow of Void Reaver power directly into her blood, before channeling it all into her palms. She poked and prodded along the Etherien Seal with the power, sifting through for the weak points of the Seal. As the ethèr crawled along the edges of the Seal, she could feel the pinch points where the Seal had bends and cracks after millennia of tampering.

Fabienne pressed against those points now. Hard. Sweat gathered at her temples as she pushed with every ounce of her might, her strength, until something popped so loud it left her ears ringing.

Fabienne pulled back, ready to celebrate her victory. But though there was a visible line fissuring through the Seal, the barrier still stood.

"What in the rotting stars..."

"So." Emmanuel's voice held amusement. "Is it my turn yet?"

Fabienne turned to glare at him.

"No."

Emmanuel grinned, and lifted his pointer finger in the air.

"You get one more try." He looked at the barrier. "Then I'm slamming into it until it breaks."

Fabienne turned back to the Etherien Seal, and closed her eyes. Something deep within her whispered. She exhaled slowly and tried again, reaching for her ethèr, but this time, she also prayed. Eyes locked on the barrier, Fabienne muttered a soft plea to Pasaille—the high heavens of all angels—hoping the Great King of the celestial heavens would hear *and* answer.

Ehyeh, if you are listening... Please. I need you. Emmanuel and I must get past this barrier. I've tried my best. But it's not enough. Please, hear me. Help me. Get us through. Thank you, Great King.

Fabienne channeled every ounce of her Void Reaving abilities again. She pressed her palms against the Etherien Seal. She pushed, one hard thrust against the barrier with all of her strength. This time, the power inside her shifted. A supernatural peace settled on her as warmth spread through her limbs, a strength unlike anything she'd felt before building inside of her. The pale glow of her ethèr deepened, became richer, denser. It no longer just shimmered—it burned. She took a deep breath, and heaved. The Seal shuddered.

Then it cracked, shattering like a thousand falling stars. A rippling shockwave of light burst outward from the depths, splintering the dark energy apart. The Seal trembled, groaned one more time, then—

It collapsed in on itself.

Emmanuel floated forward, staring, wide-eyed and silent, his jaw hanging.

Fabienne lowered her hands, her breath coming fast. The presence was gone. But the weight of it remained.

Emmanuel finally found his voice. "What in the stars did you do?"

She ignored him, shaking off the strange sensation coursing through her. "Come on. We want to be far away from here before anything comes out."

Emmanuel narrowed his gaze, hovering beside her as she turned.

"You prayed, didn't you?"

Fabienne grabbed her satchel, tossed Emmanuel his, and began flying across the new divide.

"And?"

Emmanuel scoffed, flying ahead to cut her off.

"No, no, no. That wasn't normal. You prayed and suddenly your ethèr broke through an Etherien Seal?"

"Shut up, Emmanuel." Fabienne kept flying, feeling her cheeks flush.

He grinned. "I think you're Etherien-blessed."

Fabienne glared at him, jutting out her chin. "I think you're insufferable."

He cackled but said nothing in return.

Together, they pressed forward, falling into a mutual silence, rushing to be as far away from the divide as fast as possible. Fabienne followed Emmanuel, trusting he'd memorized the Noirmother's map well enough to get them to the river without any problems. They flew for several hôrs, weaving up and down through endless, bare, and deadened branches. The Craven Wood was lifeless except for whatever hid in the shadows. Fabienne and Emmanuel pushed themselves. Neither had said a word, but both knew they didn't want to spend another dusk in the Wood.

As the hôrs of the dawn went by, Fabienne could finally smell a different scent in the air.

Water.

When they reached the clearing, the sight before them stopped them both cold.

A boat rested against the shoreline, its structure crafted from obsidian and bone. The night-like river itself glowed faintly, its surface swirling with an unnatural luminescence. And waiting beside it stood a hooded figure. They were tall and draped in layers of dark, flowing fabric. The figure's wings—if they could even be called that—were skeletal, shifting like tattered remnants of something once great. They inclined their head slightly, and though their face remained hidden, Fabienne felt the weight of their gaze. A voice, soft but hollow, echoed from beneath the hood.

"I am the Portal Keeper. I have been waiting for you, Void Reaver, Fabienne Evruel and Pandemir, Emmanuel Alfonse. Your toll has already been paid. Come and I will bring you to Takari, the home of the Taétàn giants."

CHAPTER 19
FABIENNE

Fabienne Evruel knew the Noirmother didn't send her and Emmanuel on some easy errand to find Désakré. But floating just outside of the Craven Wood's edge, while suspiciously eyeing the Portal Keeper, she was beginning to question both the danger and madness of this mission.

Fabienne and Emmanuel exchanged glances while silently debating if they would take the boat or run. Neither of them made to move first. When they refused to move closer to the boat, without another word to either of them, the Portal Keeper turned and glided onto the boat.

Fabienne considered flying back into the Craven Wood and searching for another solution. But she knew, they had none. This was their only option.

Emmanuel's grunt beside her let her know he'd just come to the same conclusion. Left with no other choice, after exchanging another look, Fabienne and Emmanuel floated onto the boat after the Keeper.

The moment they were securely on, the river swallowed the sound of the world behind them. The river itself was deathly quiet. Nothing stirred the dark waters. Everything behind them vanished instantly, like a veil falling down, and all that remained was the oppressive silence of the river and the Portal Keeper.

Fabienne stood still, her wings tucked tight against her back as her boots pressed into the cold, obsidian surface of the boat. Emmanuel stood beside her, unusually quiet, his gaze fixed ahead as the skeletal figure moved to the front. Fabienne fought not to fidget. Immediately she began calculating her options should anything go wrong. Outside of herself, Emmanuel, and the Portal Keeper, there was nothing else to be found on the boat. As if everything had been glamoured with a power that kept them blind from what was really there.

Fabienne felt a stirring in the air that made her tense. Next to her, Emmanuel began to shift uncomfortably. The river itself was… unnatural. Its surface glowed faintly, a swirling mix of midnight and moonlight, but beneath that glow… something stirred.

“I don't like this,” Emmanuel muttered.

Fabienne glanced his way and found him looking in every direction, memorizing each detail, committing it all to memory. He, too, was searching for a way out in case they would need it.

“Neither do I,” Fabienne offered, her eyes scanning the surface of the river. She didn’t trust this place. "Something's not right."

“Not at all.” His eyes were glued to the river's surface now—the honey and amber darkening to molten pools of gold. “Be prepared for anything, Fabienne. Noirmother Alexandria said nothing about what we might face out here. I wouldn't put it past her to have us tested while we're at our most vulnerable.”

Fabienne knew he was right. The Noirmother was never to be trusted. And neither was this Portal Keeper. Her thumb brushed the hilt of her dagger as she kept an eye on the Keeper and another on the surface of the river.

"Portal Keeper," Fabienne called out. "How long is our journey to Takari?"

The Portal Keeper stayed silent so long, she didn't think he would answer her.

Then a hollow voice sounded unpleasantly close to her ear.

"As long as it takes," came the bony whisper. "First, you must survive."

"Burning *rot*," Emmanuel cursed below his breath. "I knew the Noirmother set us up, I knew it!"

Fabienne shared his ire. "Look, whatever madness the Noirmother set up for us, we'll deal with it. We have to get to those catacombs."

Emmanuel went on cursing under his breath, visibly enraged at the Fraetèn Boss's dangerous games. What did the Keeper mean by *first you must survive*?

Survive *what*?

Fabienne kept her eyes peeled, every part of her alert and focused as the boat made its way down the river. Slowly, after several hôrs of travel, the air grew colder. A chill crawled along Fabienne's skin, and her ethèr stirred instinctively, sensing the shift before she did.

"Emmanuel..." She called his name, a sinking feeling twisting thick knots in her stomach.

"I feel it," Emmanuel quipped, slipping closer to her side, his eyes narrowing as the river's glow dimmed… and then flickered. He shuffled closer still, if that was even possible, his wings spreading to come up behind and around her. "We're not alone."

Fabienne's wings twitched. The light around them was beginning to fade.

Then.

"Fabienne…" Emmanuel's voice was a low growl, the rumble from his throat burning along the columns of her arms and spine.

She followed his gaze, and her hearts stopped. The glow beneath the water was gone.

And the silence of the river was like a roar. Loud, oppressive, and berating.

"Oh stars, what have we been thrown into..." Fabienne whispered, her fingers tightening around her dagger.

The Portal Keeper said nothing, continuing to guide the boat along as if nothing was happening. He never once looked back at them, or felt the need to give them any sort of warning. They were on their own.

"Rot, rot, *rot,*" Emmanuel cursed, every muscle in his body tense, ready to spring into action at any moment.

A ripple danced across the surface of the river. Just one.

Then something stirred beneath the surface.

Not one. But many somethings.

Fabienne's breath hitched. "Emmanuel…"

It was too late. A shape broke through the surface. And lunged.

Fabienne screamed, a wave of terror seizing her

limbs. She felt paralyzed, unable to move as the grotesque thing threw itself at her. Then Emmanuel's wings were there, shielding her, while swiping through the creature in one clean arc. Fabienne trembled, unable to hide her rising panic and fear.

What in the burning stars was that?

More shadows began popping out from the depths, breaking through the river's surface.

Fabienne made herself look at them, despite her rattled nerves. She forced herself to see what they were. Never in all her cycles had she heard of a creature like this. They weren't angels. They weren't fully alive. They were mere fragments of whatever they'd once been. Their bodies were disjointed beyond recognition. Their faces were distorted by agony. By fury. By vengeance. They had broken, shredded things for wings, and those eyes… The sockets were empty.

"I have never..." Emmanuel gasped, baffled by the sight, a rare sort of shock coloring his face a darker shade of brown, turning his ebony skin nearly dark like the river.

"I think... I think these... things, are bound, Emmanuel," Fabienne whispered.

"Bound to what?" Emmanuel's voice was strained in a way she'd never heard it before. And that made her nervous.

“The river,” she whispered, leaning closer to him. “Don't you see? I think they’re a part of it.”

“You’re saying the river’s alive?”

“No.” Fabienne’s stomach twisted as another shadow rose from the depths, its hollow gaze locking onto hers. “I’m saying the river is hungry.”

CHAPTER 20
FABIENNE

"If these things start attacking us, we're dead," Emmanuel hissed. "If we survive, Noir-mother Alexandria will pay for this."

Fabienne could hear the panic in his voice. Could hear the anxiety mounting. She felt the same within herself. She never for a moment thought going after the stone meant trying to fight off the undead. At a loss for what to do, she floated closer to Emmanuel, pressing fully into his side, and closed her eyes against the nightmares rising from the dark.

Another shadow lurched from the watery depths, shrieking, the piercing sound echoing in her bones. Fabienne had no strength to fight with these... *things*. So again, she dove within, and said a quick prayer to Ehyeh.

When she was forced to accept this quest, it was

to get the stone, with the hopes of earning salvation for herself and Tatiana. She couldn't lose all of that now because the Noirmother somehow found it funny to send them across a river full of vindictive spirits with no eternal holding place.

Ehyeh, please. It's me... again. I've been doing too much, I know. I've gone too far, I know. My hands are filthy and my spirit is soaked in the grime of my sins. I know. But, please, make these creatures go away. I've no clue what they are, I don't want to know, and Emmanuel and I must make it to Takari. I have to get Désakré. Please, help us. I know I don't deserve it but we need you... Again. Thank you.

Fabienne opened her eyes and found the river instantaneously still and empty. Emmanuel had swiped through the shadow that lunged before she prayed. But now, every last one of them were gone. And at the head of the boat, the Portal Keeper had turned, and was watching her from beneath his hood.

"You were supposed to survive," came his bony, chilly whisper. "You were not supposed to hail the aid of the Great King."

"Then you should've made that clear *before* we got onto this stars-forsaken boat."

Fabienne looked around and found the sôlsunes beginning to light the sky overhead. The darkness of the river seemed lighter now. It was still obsidian, but not as menacing as it was just moments ago.

She couldn't believe her luck. Ehyeh had come through for her. Immediately. Twice. Maybe she'd have to visit the Temple and pay some kind of homage to give proper thanksgiving. It had been so long since she'd been. Especially because a thief like herself had no business going inside a place so sacred. But maybe she could sneak in, late one dusknite, and give the Great King a proper thank you.

Assuming she survived this foul quest.

"I see the image of a portal in the distance, Keeper," Emmanuel bellowed from beside her. "Onwards! We won't be on this blasted thing longer than we must. To Takari!"

The Portal Keeper said no more, still eyeing Fabienne warily. She couldn't guess his thoughts. His face was obscured and well hidden by the hood of his cloak. She wondered at what game he was playing. Maybe he wasn't even in league with the Noirmother. Maybe this little test had another purpose.

Whatever the Portal Keeper was up to, Fabienne was too tired to dwell on it. They had a powerful stone to find and procure before the other rogues found it first.

Fabienne remained at the edge of the obsidian boat, staring into the thick, swirling mist that veiled the river's surface. The air was damp, heavy with an eerie stillness, the water beneath them as black as the void. The very essence of it pressed against her senses, gnawing at the edges of her consciousness. She couldn't wait to be far away from it.

The Portal Keeper stood at the bow, silent and still. His presence was an unnatural weight, one that seemed to press against Fabienne's ribs, making it difficult to breathe. She wondered where he'd come from. How did he become the Portal Keeper? Who traveled these waters and how often? Her mind wandered near and far as the trip grew solemn, but not peaceful. She was still wary of the water. She kept close to Emmanuel, just in case. So far, as time passed, nothing else happened.

It seemed the further the boat went, they were nowhere nearer to the portal entry of Takari. Stars. She didn't think she'd last on this rotting boat much longer.

Then—

"Portal Keeper, this silence is insufferable. Would you tell us a story? And please, for stars sake, make it a good one."

Fabienne whipped her head to the side, glaring. "Emmanuel," she hissed. "Now is not the time. Don't."

He smirked, ignoring her entirely, floating forward lazily, arms crossed. His confidence was a mask. She could see the tension in his shoulders, the way his wings were held just a little too stiffly. He was just as unsettled as she was. Yet, he was still trying to push the Portal Keeper.

Fool.

"Come now, don't be a hoarder." Emmanuel continued, tilting his head. "You seem to have an abundance of tales to share. I promise we..." A quick glance her way, then back to the creature. "*I* am a good listener." Fabienne's nostrils flared at his subtle jab. "Tell your tale. I will listen, and try not to ask too many questions."

The Portal Keeper said nothing. He didn't acknowledge Emmanuel or his taunts. His stillness began to unnerve Fabienne. Something in her gut twisted. Emmanuel shouldn't have pushed the Keeper. She slipped close to Emmanuel, trying to tug on his leathers to pull him back.

"Maybe he should be left alone—"

An eerie mist swirled around the Portal Keeper like living tendrils, shifting with each unspoken breath. The air on the boat, and all around them, began growing colder. Thicker.

"Oh, *stars*," Fabienne whispered.

Then the Portal Keeper moved.

Fabienne had no time to react before a sound careened in the air. It wasn't speech. It wasn't anything she'd ever heard before. It was a scraping of existence, a distortion of reality itself. The boat groaned as the air around them collapsed inward, bending under the sheer force of the sound. The weight of it struck Fabienne's chest like an invisible blow, her wings tightening against her back as her breath hitched. Her body was flung from Emmanuel, tossed to the side. She gasped, vision blurring. Something in the air cracked, like thunder splitting the sky.

When Fabienne lifted her head, she found Emmanuel on the floor of the boat, his face aghast. His usually cocky grin was gone, replaced by an expression Fabienne had never seen before. Pure, unadulterated, fear. Emmanuel twitched, his wings jerking awkwardly, as his eyes seemed to be staring at something that wasn't there.

The space around the Portal Keeper continued to unravel, moving between shapes and forms Fabienne couldn't comprehend. The being had no defined edges, its hooded form twisting, expanding. Then, in an instant, everything fell silent except for Fabienne and Emmanuel's ragged breathing.

Fabienne inhaled sharply, while her body convulsed. It took several deep breaths to get her hearts to slow, and her mind to calm back down. She forced herself to blink, to steady her hands.

Emmanuel's face was pale, his gaze frozen on something she couldn't see. For once, he had nothing to say. Without thinking, Fabienne pushed to her feet and floated to him. She pulled him up, as he shook his head to clear away whatever nightmare had gripped him. She reached for him, her fingers intertwining with his. To her surprise, Emmanuel gripped back, squeezing her hand.

Fabienne leaned her head on Emmanuel's shoulder, holding his arm tight with her free hand. He brushed her knuckles with his thumb, letting his wings rise to come around her like a protective shield. For the rest of the journey, neither let go of the other. They stayed that way, unmoving, eyes glued to the Portal Keeper and the river, as they slowly drew nearer to the portal entry of Takari.

Finally the Portal Keeper spoke.

"We are here."

Fabienne blinked, utterly confused. She could've sworn she thought there was a portal in the distance. A rip of the realms between the Gamarh Elstar and the moon ring of Takari that encircled the massive planet.

Instead, it was like they'd been brought to a thin veil. Nothing seemed out of the ordinary. They were still on the river. And there certainly didn't seem to be a crossing between worlds.

"Where the rot is *here*?" Emmanuel said low, wary, unsure if the Portal Keeper would strike him again.

The Portal Keeper made the slightest movement. The wave of a hand. Then it seemed like the atèmos themselves were zooming by. One moment, Fabienne felt like she had been flung into the galactic starry scape. The next, she'd landed on the wrong side of her wings in an altogether foreign place.

And the Portal Keeper was nowhere to be found.

CHAPTER 21

FABIENNE

"Where in the stars—"

"Oh my goodness, Emmanuel look!" Fabienne screeched, her throat going dry. She pointed ahead. "It's the Catacombs of the Taétàn Kings."

"But how..."

Fabienne didn't hear anything else he said. Her eyes were glued to the city perched in the opposite direction. The grand city, and home, to billions of Taétàn giants.

Fabienne looked at their high towers of stone, and intricately carved palaces, each detail so defined they could be noticed from this vantage point. She watched, heightening her angelic vision for a better look, as the giants strolled around in their lush clothings of purple and gold, their velvet capes, odd armor-like headdresses, and proud grins. They were so far, but if felt as if she was in the middle of their city, walking among them.

Each one was a bill of health. After all, they lured angels in, drained their fôrs and ethèr, and used it to fuel their cities and keep their giants alive and well.

The air here was heavy, laced with a scent she couldn't place—something between the dampness of old stone and the metallic tang of blood. It was like Xodom, yet so completely different. The world of the giants. A contrast to her own world of angels.

A roiling rage began churning through her body, the anger flooding her blood, her bones, and coloring her vision scarlet. These were the beings who'd seduced her sisari. Had manipulated her into coming here. They'd gotten her to fall in love with one of their giants, then he'd given her a disease even an angel couldn't survive. Her life for theirs.

Fabienne hated the Taétàn with a force that could color all of Xodom in pitch, and now, floating in the world of giants, she'd give anything to light them all on fire, and watch every last one of them burn.

"Fabienne."

She didn't respond. Her eyes were glued to the giants and how freely they moved about their world, as if their kind hadn't devastated her own. Tatiana was all she had left, and because of the Taétàn, she might lose her sisari, too. She hated that the sôlsunes shined here, just like they did in Xodom. It wasn't fair. The giants didn't deserve anything good in any of the realms. They deserved to rot.

A large palm, oddly gentle in its touch, landed on her shoulder. Squeezed. Another palm curled around her waist, slowly, tenderly, drawing her attention away from the city of the Taétàn.

Fabienne felt her cheeks wet. It wasn't until she brushed them with a finger, that she realized she'd been crying. A sort of raw, desperate cry, that burned, and raged, and demanded to heard. Demanded to be avenged.

Fabienne looked up at Emmanuel. His gaze held no judgement. Only understanding, and a deep resolve. Fabienne wondered in that moment, when they found the stone, would he give it to her?

As Emmanuel held her gaze, a rush of heat flooded her chest. She felt hot, disoriented, and heady. She felt... *seen.* And safe. And though that terrified her, all she wanted was to lean closer to his tempestuous edge, and fall.

For once, someone looked at her, not to demand, or take, or break. He looked at her with knowing and a primal need to fix it. This wasn't the first time he'd had this look, even though he played it off well. Now she saw something else in his eyes, and it made her feel something she couldn't put into words.

Emmanuel broke away first, and thank the stars for it. Fabienne felt foolish. She had to focus. They were here. They'd made it to Takari. Now they had one last thing to do. Get the stone, and get the rot out.

The Catacombs of the Taétàn Kings stretched out before them.

Fabienne took a slow, measured breath, scanning their surroundings. There were no Watchers. No sentries. Nothing. The entrance loomed, flanked by statues of grotesque figures that seemed more warped by time. Their blank eyes stared forward, their faces carved into expressions of torment and sorrow.

Fabienne's wings twitched uneasily in the column of her spine. The six membranous pairs anxiously reacted to the unnatural stillness.

"We're finally here," she breathed. "And we're completely on our own."

Emmanuel, floating beside her, nodded, eyes taking in the entrance to the catacombs. "We've always been on our own, my pretty little thief." He glanced her way. He tossed her his usual, careless grin that had grown to bring her comfort. "Let's move."

Fabienne met his gaze, searching for any sign of

hesitation in his eyes, the amber shining in contrast to the honey, but found none. He was pressing forward, as always, reckless and willing to gamble even when the odds were impossibly stacked against him.

Fabienne nodded once, then she pushed off the ground, her wings spreading wide as she ascended into the cavernous mouth of the tombs.

Darkness greeted them like an old friend. The catacombs stretched out and *down.* The more they flew, the deeper they descended. It went on endlessly beneath them, tunnels upon tunnels, with layers of stone that vanished into the abyss. The walls, carved from dark marble, were lined with sarcophagi, each adorned with elaborate engravings of Taétàn royalty, those who served the royals, and warriors alike.

"This feels too easy," Fabienne whispered. "Not a Watcher in sight. Why?"

"You miss the stiff-necked enforcers already?" Emmanuel's voice was light, but he sounded more cautious than usual.

"I just don't understand how there isn't even one Taétàn here, keeping a watch. This isn't making sense."

"I didn't realize anything about this whole quest was supposed to make sense."

Fabienne shot him a glare. Emmanuel grinned,

back. They kept flying, as her eyes darted between the dark corridors stretching below them. The silence pressed in on them, suffocating her.

Fabienne felt movement in the air, and she stiffened. Her wings faltered slightly, her hands clenching into fists. She looked around, scanning the expanse of tombs below. Nothing moved. No shadows. No footsteps. And yet—

Her wings rose, all six pairs spreading, ready to defend and attack. Emmanuel drifted closer, but said nothing, his wings spreading slightly as if shielding her from behind. The movement was subtle, but it didn't go unnoticed. Fabienne forced herself to keep flying, but her pulse thrummed wildly.

"If what the Crescent showed me was correct, we're almost there," Emmanuel's voice was barely above a whisper. "Keep moving, but be ready for anything. I don't think we're alone in here after all."

Fabienne didn't argue.

They flew in tight formation, Fabienne slightly ahead, Emmanuel just behind. Her eyes flickered from corridor to corridor, her ears straining for even the faintest sound beyond their own movements. The closer they got to the heart of the catacombs, the deeper the darkness they descended into grew. Down ahead, nestled into a vast chasm of unending darkness and gloom, a grand chamber loomed, more massive than any they had passed.

"Oh my stars," Fabienne exclaimed. "Is that..."

"I do believe we have reached the grave of the Taétàn King."

CHAPTER 22

FABIENNE

Fabienne hovered just outside the Taétàn King's chamber, her breath catching in her throat. She was speechless. She had stolen from many of status and wealth throughout Xodom, completing job after another for the Ukaveli Syndicate. She was used to seeing an obscene amount of riches, all hoarded into one place, as a symbol of power and long-lasting rule among the angels.

But this? She was blown away by the grave of Takari's former king.

The tomb of the Taétàn king was beyond anything she'd imagined. It wasn't just a burial site. The grave was a vault of history, power, and reverence. Whoever had been responsible for designing the grave, then bringing it to life, had done an immaculate job. Though the tomb seemed empty, there had to be someone who maintained its upkeep.

Everything was orderly and in their rightful place. There were gifts bestowed upon the king perched by his sarcophagus. An immeasurable amount of treasure was strewn throughout the grave.

The grand hall stretched endlessly with towering black marble columns inlaid with veins of glowing gold. Their surfaces were engraved with ancient etchings of Taétàn lore. The ceiling was a dome of dark crystal, flickering with lights that mimicked a starry sky.

The air was thick with the scent of time itself—aged metal, stone dust, and something faintly sweet, like incense burned long ago and never quite faded.

She should have been focused on their mission. Get in, get the stone, get out. She should have been scanning for traps, listening for movement. But for a moment, all she could do was marvel.

Row upon row of treasures sprawled across the chamber. Elaborate chests overflowed with gemstones. Weapons had been crafted with such delicate precision. They looked more like works of art than tools of war. Golden relics were adorned with sacred markings. And at the center of it all, on a grand obsidian dais, lay the sarcophagus of the Taétàn king.

It was enormous, befitting one of the, physically, largest giants to have ever existed in Takari's history. The coffin itself was laden in black and gold, adorned with monstrous figures carved in frozen agony, their faces contorted as if they had been trapped in suffering for eternity. The lid, sculpted from a slab of pure dark quartz, shimmered faintly in the dim light of the chamber.

Fabienne almost missed the change in the air, as if something had been awakened, and was lurking about to see who was responsible. The darkness grew heavy, weighing down her focus. Her resolve. She found her breaths turned shallow. Slow. Ragged. Like she'd been flying at full speed and hadn't a chance to catch her breath. But how could that be? She'd barely done a thing.

There was a growing absence of certainty all around. Fabienne felt for sure, something was lurking, and she'd have to fight her way out of these catacombs if she was going to survive. The shadows at the edges of the chamber lengthened, stretching unnaturally as if reaching for her. She felt them, deep in her bones, curling at the edge of her senses.

Fabienne exhaled, steadying herself, and floating into the chamber. "This is it."

Emmanuel landed beside her, arms crossed. "Looks like the giants fancy their trinkets like angels do. Good to know greed isn't exclusive to us." He chuckled darkly, but there was no mirth in it. "Now we just have to take what we came for."

Fabienne narrowed her eyes, scanning the sarcophagus. "I don't think we should rush this. we need to be careful. We could touch something, and set off an unfortunate chain of events."

"Fabienne," He flashed her a grin. "You know that *I'm* not the careful one, right?" He wriggled his brows. "I don't care about any of this precaution. We're on the dance floor of the dead. We find the stone, and we get the rot out of here."

Fabienne wanted to argue, but Emmanuel turned from her, effectively ending the conversation. She flinched at his attitude, but shook it off. Fine, then. She side-stepped him, gliding forward, her body rigid with tension. Everything in her was telling her this was a trap.

A sudden chill snaked up her spine. She stopped mid-step, eyes flicking to the shadows stretching along the chamber's perimeter. The hint of light from the tomb's golden walls didn't seem to reach those corners. The darkness was unnatural, grating against her skin. Her fingers curled instinctively, ready to summon her ethèr.

There was a faint noise behind her. A whisper of movement. Something had moved across the threshold. Fabienne snapped her wings out, pivoting, scanning the darkness—

But there was nothing. Just empty tombs and empty corridors. Nothing but silence met her.

She turned back, only to find Emmanuel watching her, his expression unreadable. His blades were in his hands. She hadn't even heard him pull them out.

"I think we have company, my pretty little thief," he said quietly. "And not the angelic sort."

Fabienne shivered. After what they faced in the Craven Wood and on the river, she was done dealing with the undead.

Emmanuel tilted his head toward the sarcophagus. "We need to move."

They crossed the chamber together, floating lightly. Fabienne's wings twitched involuntarily. She neared the sarcophagus and lowered herself to the stone floor without a sound. She felt like she was back in the Armand Palàs. Stealth would be her friend here.

"Okay, how do you want to do this? I don't mind going up and checking first. The sarcophagus doesn't look like its been moved in many cycles, but I can use my ethèr to pop it open and get us access. Hopefully without triggering anything else."

Silence.

Fabienne whipped around to glare at Emmanuel. Now was not the time for him to give her the silent treatment. It was then Fabienne learned, Emmanuel was no longer beside her.

A scrape of stone sounded. The sound was a deafening roar in the silence of the catacombs. Anyone looking for them would know *exactly* where to look.

Fabienne opened her mouth to scold Emmanuel, and froze. Her hearts slammed against her ribs. The sarcophagus was wide open.

And Emmanuel floated above it, holding Désakré in his hand.

The stone was nothing like she'd imagined. It wasn't a stone at all. Désakré was a shrunken star that seemed to be... dormant. Waiting to be awakened. It was a small, gilded sphere, pulsing with a blueish-and-ivory radiance. And something inside the star was pulsing with life. The moment Fabienne's eyes landed on it, her ethèr recoiled.

"Emmanuel—"

She looked into his eyes and flinched at what she saw there. Wonder, greed, pride, arrogance. Hadn't she thought, just outside of the catacombs, that maybe he'd find Désakré and give it to her? Hadn't they had an understanding of sorts?

The cocky sneer filling his face said something

different. She'd gotten soft, fallen for his charm, and he'd played her for a fool.

Stupid. She was so burning stupid.

They had never been allies. But she had been an idiot to think he'd be anything but her enemy. She should've gotten to Désakré first. Rotting idiot that she was.

Now she'd have to fight the Domenent to get it. Because only one of them could have it. And she would burning well make sure it was her.

"Drop it, Emmanuel."

Emmanuel's amber-and-honey eyes were different now. They had darkened, dilated, and now his expression was caught somewhere between awe and madness. He didn't look like his usual self. His grip on the star was tight, knuckles blanching, as if he had no intention of letting it go. Ever. Power coiled around him, licking at his skin, tendrils of shadow and light intertwining like something sentient. He was so rotting handsome. The shadows began to curl around his frame, making the red of his locs and short beard look like scarlet fire. She wanted to tackle him, but she had to be smart about it. Especially because they had no idea what the star could do if it was no longer dormant.

Fabienne's chest tightened. "Put it down. Now."

Emmanuel looked at her. And he smiled. A slow,

almost lazy grin. And burn her if it didn't set her on fire inside in a way that made it difficult to think straight. She cursed her traitorous body.

"Now Fabienne, I've grown to know you to be a sensible Domenent." His voice was low, sensual, almost like a delicious purr that sent a chill skittering down her spine. "We talked about this, didn't we? Besides. You don't really expect for me to part with the star, do you? And what a beautiful surprise. A star, not a stone after all."

Fabienne's wings flared, instinct screaming at her. "You need to let it go. Now."

Emmanuel exhaled. Then he burst out laughing. He actually tilted his head back, and full on cackled.

Fabienne's emotions felt raw. The betrayal stung, though she'd known it would be coming. That was their deal after all. Whoever got to it first.

Tatiana would not survive, all her efforts were going to fail, and it was going to be her fault. She'd planned for so many variables, and yet. She hadn't planned for him. *Again.*

Emmanuel's ethèr surged, raw and unchecked, slamming into the chamber like a tidal wave. His wings snapped open, six pairs of black, membranous limbs casting deep, rippling shadows. Then he slammed his wings down.

Darkness rushed out from him in a violent wave, swallowing the chamber whole. It crashed into Fabienne like a cold tide, forcing her back, snuffing out the glow of the Taétàn's relics.

For a moment, there was nothing. No sight. No sound.

Just a void.

Fabienne fought against it, trying to summon her ethèr, but the dark had weight, pulling, consuming. It pressed against her skin, against her mind, whispering in a voice she didn't understand. Her breath came in short gasps, her vision flickering as she strained against the force. Then, just as suddenly, it was over. The shadows peeled away, dispersing like mist burned by dawn.

Fabienne stumbled forward, disoriented, wings snapping to steady herself. Her vision adjusted, the chamber flickering back into dim clarity.

When she looked around, she was alone.

Emmanuel, and the star, were gone.

CHAPTER 23
EMMANUEL

Emmanuel Alfonse hated himself for double-crossing Fabienne the way he'd just done. Even worse, he couldn't even control it. *As if she'd believe that.*

As they'd descended into the catacombs together, he had been driven by two thoughts: Get the stone. Then, give it to Fabienne.

The look she had on her face when she'd stared out at Takari in the distance had unraveled something inside of him. She'd laid eyes on the world of the Taétàn giants and had been undone. Instantly he knew, her broken, feral rage had been something he wanted to take from her. It was a stupid idea, but he'd made up his mind about it.

Then his eyes fell on Désakré.

An unnatural force had entered inside of him and

lurched for the star. It gripped his mind and tried quenching the inner light in his hearts. It was a compulsion he had no control over. He'd meant to take the star and give it to her. Now he was driven by a need to keep it for himself, no matter the cost.

Emmanuel flew hard and fast, losing Fabienne to the darkness he'd created. He pulled on his ethèr, feeling the hum of his Pandemir powers warming his blood. He raced through the catacombs, turning corner after corner, driven—not by his own volition —to get out with the star and race off with the treasure.

Emmanuel raced past the gargantuan onyx columns upholding the catacombs, an unnatural rhythm beating in his chest. Stars, what was happening? Why couldn't he control himself?

He weaved through the dark, navigating expertly across its wide chasms in the low light, flying *up* to get out.

A soft chuckle made him pull up short. He didn't feel them until he was already surrounded. When Emmanuel looked up, he found himself face to face with Noirmother Alexandria.

"How in the hèls—"

"Well done, dear Vagabond. I knew you were the right dog to tell fetch." She smiled, cold and cruel, something dark flashing in her eyes. "A shame. I do think our little Reaver was starting to fancy you. But as they say, once a Vagabond, always a Vagabond." She opened her palm. "Do be a good doggo, and hand over the star."

Emmanuel cursed his carelessness. He'd flown straight into an ambush and didn't realize it until it was too late. He was surrounded. His only consolation was that he was alone. If Fabienne noticed what was happening, she could at least get away before getting caught.

Emmanuel surveyed the chamber and calculated his odds.

They were slim, but he would fight his way through anyway.

The Noirmother floated at the center of this new chamber in the catacombs, blocking his way to the other side, calm as ever, her eyes glinting with something murderous. Behind her was a mix of Fraetèn and Taétàn. But no Crescents. Thank the burning stars. Emmanuel didn't care about the giants. He could easily plow through them, even if they were as big as him. But the Fraetèn... rot. There was a lot of them.

And behind the lot were three Faedes. Emmanuel's stomach curdled like old, unsatisfying angel-wine. He'd spent cycles outrunning these Fallen. Dodging their marks, slipping through their fingers, staying a breath ahead of their grasp. They'd always managed to track him down, no matter how often he moved around and stuck to the shadows—but he'd never gotten caught. Until now, thanks to the Noirmother. He hoped she'd rot in the lowest pits of the Hèls.

"You really are one for dramatics," Emmanuel said with a grin at her.

She gave him a small smile, but her cold eyes told him she was tired of this game. She wanted the star, and she'd kill him for it. The Noirmother flexed her hand. And all at once, the Fraetèn angels, giants, and fallen angels, *moved.*

Emmanuel dove deep into his fôrs, drowning in his well of ethèr. He summoned every ounce of his Pandemir power, knowing he'd need every bit if he'd have a chance at surviving this. A group of Fraetèn and Taétàn lunged at him, daggers and clubs unsheathed, ready to cut him through.

Then Fabienne was there, bulldozing through them like boulders crashing through tree limbs. She seethed, her shoulders strained with unleashed fury. Her hatred for the Taétàn and Fraetèn was evident. The impact was brutal.

Fabienne moved like a storm—fluid, unyielding, and overwhelming. The Taétàn were larger, but Fabienne was an angel. She was stronger, and she knew it.

She cut the giants down with a viciousness that was deliciously satisfying.

Fabienne threw herself at the swinging Fraetèn, knocking through them with an unsettling ease. Emmanuel realized she could only be doing so because her rage at their presence must have momentarily eclipsed her fury at his betrayal.

One of the Taétàn tried to grab her. She twisted midair, slammed a foot into his jaw, then shoved her blade straight through the weak point in is armor. Another came at her from the side—she ducked, spread her wings, and used the force to propel herself upward, bringing her knee into his skull with enough force to crack it open.

Emmanuel could have floated there and watched. She was terrifying. Lethal. *Beautiful.* But then a Faede moved toward him, and he was forced back into reality.

"Yeah, I don't think so," Emmanuel said. He twisted out of the way as the Faede lunged, its form flickering between corporeal and shadow. He countered with a bone crunching punch filled with ethèr, then sent a shockwave outward that blasted the creature back. The Fallen hissed in anguish, bearing its hideous claws at him.

Emmanuel spun, his ethèr surging outward. A deep rumble shook the catacombs as he slammed his wings down, creating an explosion of raw force that sent several of the Fraetèn stumbling back. The catacomb's walls cracked, dust and stone raining from above. He slammed a fist into the ground to trigger a quake through the catacombs, sending a concentrated wave of ethèr slicing through the space, severing several of the Taétàn's weapons in half.

Fabienne was a blur of precision, slicing through opponents, dodging, and countering. Emmanuel wasn't as elegant, and he preferred it that way. He had always been a bit messy, unpolished, all instinct and cunning. It was what gave him the edge he often used to win in combat. He was unpredictable and chaotic at every turn. Still, no matter how hard they fought, the Fraetèn and Taétàn kept coming, and the Faedes were unfazed.

Looming behind it all, the Noirmother watched, waiting for the perfect moment to strike.

"Fabienne!" he shouted, dodging a blade meant for his throat. "We've gotta go. *Now*. Follow me!"

He didn't wait for her to listen. He took off, shooting into the dark. Only hearing the familiar pulse of her wings close behind, told him she'd listened. And from the midst of the chamber, as he pulled far away, he could hear the Noirmother sigh.

"Well, well. I was hoping we'd have some fun. Kill them, and bring me the star."

CHAPTER 24
EMMANUEL

Emmanuel flew hard, his breath ragged, his wings aching from the speed at which he and Fabienne cut through the twisting tunnels of the catacombs. The dungeon-like tombs were an insufferable thing to fly through. It was hot like a sumyrin dawn, and it stunk. The rancid odor of brimstone curled through each tunnel, making him want to gag.

Vagabond, the Fallen hissed, their voices snaking through his mind, jarring against his thoughts. *You have a debt to pay. And we do not forget. We will never forget.*

Emmanuel flew faster, unwilling to let the Faedes catch up to him. He glanced over at Fabienne. She was keeping up with him easily, her shrewd eyes taking in as much detail as she could through their flight. He wouldn't be surprised if she'd already come up with multiple ways to escape their pursuers, and kill him for his treachery, too. As they flew, they managed to lose the Fraetèn and Taétàn pretty quickly. But the Fallen continued to give chase.

The tunnels were a maze of endless dark, twisting and narrowing. Emmanuel's only hope was to divert their pursuers, long enough to make it out of the catacombs, and somehow out of Takari without being detected. Where he'd go if he survived? He hadn't thought that through yet. But if he could escape, he wasn't sure he'd go back to Xodom. He was getting tired of living in the shadows.

A hard whack to his head jostled him out of his thoughts. He snapped his head to the side to glare at Fabienne. He'd forgotten she wanted to throttle him mid-flight.

"You stole Désakré," she fumed. "Then, you got consumed by it, like some possessed freak summoned from a pocket dimension between Elledelle's realms."

She snarled, her rage causing spittle to leave her mouth. She looked feral, utterly unhinged, and irrevocably adorable beyond compare. It took everything in him to not laugh at her flushed cheeks, and swinging hands, as they angled their bodies through the catacombs.

"And *then*, you were dumb enough to fly straight into an ambush?" she shrieked. "You're the idiot of the realms, I swear it, Emmanuel! You're a rotting fool of an angel. Full of stupid decisions! We survive this? You're dead. By *my* hands," she seethed. Her nostrils flared, the winged curves of her ears twitching with her spiraling anger. He fought not to smile, but a bit of his amusement curved his lips upward, anyway.

"Dramatic. Oh, so dramatic. Have you any idea how much of my life is based on stupid decisions?" Emmanuel panted, tugging her into a sharp turn after him. "Besides, we're still breathing. Are we not?"

Fabienne shot him a glare that promised violence.

"Désakré leaves these catacombs with *me*," she hissed. An ugly sneer colored her face. Stars. She really was angry. "If I have to beat the life out of you to get it—"

Emmanuel just managed to wrench Fabienne to the side, before the wall they just flew by collapsed on itself, the stones nearly smothering them beneath rubble.

"If it's any consolation, I do want to give it to you —" Emmanuel managed, before a strange knot formed in his throat. He felt a jerk from within, like he was being pulled on a leash. He snarled, trying to shake the sensation off.

"What in the stars," Fabienne breathed, her eyes

widening at him. "Emmanuel... there are shadows snaking through your body! What's happening to—"

A wall of black, seething shadow tore through a wall right behind them. A pile of stone tumbled from above. Fabienne shoved Emmanuel out of the way. They dodged the cave-in, their wings contorting to shield their bodies from the falling debris. The unmistakable presence of the Faedes was near, pushing against their backs like a physical weight. The Fallen had gained speed and would soon be upon them.

They fell silent, a mutual understanding forming. They had to concentrate and put some serious distance between them and the Faedes. Emmanuel flew hard, pulsing each of his wings at full speed, weaving through the levels of the catacombs. He started flying up again, pushing to get higher so he could get the rot *out*.

He could hear Fabienne beside him, flying steady. She stayed close to his side, every now and again sneaking a worried glance at him. He subtly watched her as they flew. He'd spent his entire life on the run, thinking only of himself, doing everything he could to be the one youngling that survived in his bloodline. He didn't know a world, a life, where he didn't have to run. Where he didn't choose to run.

He knew Fabienne was familiar with that life, too. A blood debt to the Ukaveli was no small thing. She knew how to run. Hide. Slip in and out of the shadows. Yet, instead of taking her chances, here she was, *with him.*

Emmanuel wasn't a fool. Sure, she wanted the star. She could breathe fire all dawn about what she'd do to him to get it. But he heard the truth between her threats. She didn't come back for the star. She came back for him.

Something inside him broke at the realization.

Fabienne could've left. She could've ditched him, escaped the ambush, slipped past the Noirmother, and disappeared. After all, their hunters weren't after either of them. They were all after the star. If anyone could vanish into the shadows, it was Fabienne Evruel. And yet...

Shc stayed.

She looked at him then. Her mesmerizing pale and silver eyes meeting his molten honey-amber ones. There was something blooming there he couldn't quite name. But he had a feeling what he saw in her eyes was the same sensation coursing through his chest.

"Emmanuel," she whispered through their flight. "You're staring."

The words left his mouth before he could stop them.

"Pasari once told me, while I was still a youngling,

that I had an eye for beauty so divinely glorious I'd die before realizing looking so long would blind me for a lifetime."

Fabienne's mouth hung open in a small *o*. He noticed the fluttering of her lashes. The quick spurts of breath she took now as her face flushed. Her ears twitched, jittery with nerves and her flight hitched, just for a moment. Stars. She was resplendent. He relished in her shock, as she worked to compose herself. A breath later, she was flying steadily again. His eyes fell to her mouth, and it was an effort to wrench them back to her eyes.

"I..." Fabienne opened her mouth to say something. Then shut it again.

A new fire burned in Emmanuel's chest, raw and unfamiliar. If Fabienne was staying with him, he'd make rotting sure she survived.

They angled higher, dodging through the maze of ancient passageways. A deep, guttural growl reverberated through the catacombs.

Fabienne twisted midair. “What in the stars was that?”

Emmanuel didn’t get a chance to answer before he saw them. Hulking, twisted forms shambled from the darkness, their bald heads gleaming. Their elongated limbs twitched, and their dead eyes locked onto the two of them.

"Is that a burning Zambi?" Fabienne screeched.

Then she dove, her blades flashing. Her ethèr sparked as she severed one of the Zambi's limbs. The creature didn't react—didn't even flinch as it swung its remaining arm at her.

Emmanuel was on the creature before it could swing again. He slammed into the Zambi with the full force of his Pandemir ethèr, sending it crashing into a stone pillar. Another Zambi screeched, diving for them. Emmanuel twisted in the air, and caught its leathery throat with a single hand. He clenched, his ethèr burning hot beneath his skin, and ripped it apart. Emmanuel lifted his head and found another one charging at Fabienne. She turned sharply, just barely missing the swipe—

Then she cried out. Her golden blood splattered across the catacomb's floor.

Emmanuel's world snapped into focus, and fury detonated through his body. Fabienne faltered, clutching her side. A jagged wound tore across her ribs where a Zambi's claws had slashed through her leathers. She started bleeding out profusely.

"*NO!*" Emmanuel roared.

A feral sound left Emmanuel's throat. His ethèr surged, unchecked and violent. The shadows recoiled as his wings expanded, a force of raw, unfiltered power erupting from him. He lost himself to his rage, letting his vision turn black. He cut down through the hoard of Zambi mercilessly. Blood and bone filled the chamber. When the carnage settled, the chamber was eerily silent. Fabienne let out a shaky breath, her crumpled form unmoving.

"Burn it all," he cursed, pulling her into his arms and against his chest. "Foolish aèl."

Fabienne gave a weak chuckle. "Takes a fool to recognize a fool, I say."

Emmanuel tried to ignore the way his chest clenched at the sound of her voice.

It was soft. And too weak.

He had to get her to safety. He glanced around, scanning the ruins, his breathing labored from the fight. Not far away, he found a small refuge. A half-collapsed passage leading to a hidden chamber. Emmanuel started making his way towards it.

Fabienne grumbled in protest. "I can fly."

"No, you can't."

He slipped through the crack in the wall, the space small, tight, but safe. The moment they were inside, he lowered her gently to the stone, pressing a hand to her side to slow the bleeding. Fabienne hissed but didn't push him away. He worked quickly, tearing fabric from his leathers, pressing it into the wound. Angels could self-heal, so he wasn't too worried. But she was weak and had lost a lot of blood. He hoped her body had enough strength to repair itself, at least enough for them to make it out of the catacombs.

Emmanuel looked down at Fabienne, the dim light casting shadows across her face, her eyes dulled from blood loss. Something lodged itself in his throat.

"Why didn't you leave me?" He half whispered, half begged.

Fabienne chuckled, though she winced with pain. "What? And let you ruin everything alone? And you call me dramatic."

Something inside Emmanuel split open like a fissure through the side of a mountain. He hadn't known he needed anyone until Fabienne showed up, and refused to leave.

His grip on her tightened. Without thinking, he pulled her against him, his wings wrapping around them both. Fabienne tensed—but only for a moment. Then she let out a slow exhale, relaxing into him, resting her head against his chest, and let her eyes fall shut.

There, Emmanuel decided. He was done running. And if Fabienne would have him, he would give her all six of his wretched hearts, and then the world. With every Taétàn's head pierced on a spike.

CHAPTER 25

FABIENNE

Agony lanced through Fabienne's body the moment consciousness returned. She gasped, squealing with anguish. Her rib cage burned, her bones felt brittle, and her leathers were damp with golden blood, the acrid stench filling her nostrils. Her limbs felt leaden, and her wings twitched uselessly at her back.

Stars.

She remembered failing a job for the Ukaveli once. The job was supposed to be simple. Break into the treasury of Xodom's finest bank, steal a prestigious crest, get out and keep it quiet. When she'd failed—not to get the crest, but to keep the job quiet—the Ukaveli boss had her stripped down to her shift, and beaten so badly she couldn't move for three wèks.

The pain nipping at every ligament in her body now, was worse than that beating. But, she was alive. That, in itself, was a miracle.

Fabienne exhaled, feeling the slow flow of breath exiting her lungs. Her breathing was labored, and her chest felt constricted. That wasn't good. She tried remembering what had happened. Emmanuel had been ambushed by the Noirmother. There had been fighting with Fraetèn, Taétàn, and stars, even Faedes. Then they'd fled. But then there were Zambi. And she'd been struck. Badly. The memories raced through her mind, a barrage of terror, panic, fear, and a ruthless determination to survive.

"Burning hèls," she wheezed, curling into a ball as another wave of pain snaked through her entire body. The agony was endless.

After a few deep breaths, Fabienne gingerly lengthened her limbs, stretching her body. A soft moan escaped her lips at the slightest give of relief through her battered body. Beneath her was something firm, but still warm and altogether inviting. She adjusted herself so she could settle down more comfortably. She moved her hands around, feeling for what she was sprawled on. Then she remembered Emmanuel had scooped her up, tucked her away in a hidden chamber, and held her close. And not for a moment had he let her go.

Instantly a spike of heat set her cheeks ablaze.

Oh, burning stars.

Fabienne tilted her head back, and found the cunning eyed, handsome angel looking down at her, still in his arms. She jerked, rushing to sit up and pull away from him, but her body protested, her muscles screaming out. As quickly as she sat up, she leaned back down, curling in Emmanuel's lap with a sigh.

"Careful."

His voice was low, steady, and close. His breath curled around the winged tip of her ear, sending a delicious tremor through her upper body. Emmanuel's arms were wrapped around her waist like a vice. He held her with a gentleness that was completely at odds with his brutish strength. He pushed back a few of her loose locs, tucking them behind her ear.

"You've healed some," he said, his voice husky, making her heady. "But you need to heal a bit more before we move on. That devilish creature did more damage than I thought."

Fabienne shifted in Emmanuel's lap to get a better look at him. He was leaning back against the stone wall, his gaze trained on her with an intensity that set all six of her heats beating wildly. His reddish, short-cropped locs were disheveled, his new growth evident on the shaved sides, as his eyes brimmed with concern and immeasurable, heated passion. His beard had also grown beyond its short trim, the reddish coils filling his face.

"I'm feeling better," she said, not wanting to concern him further. "We can start moving again."

He snorted. "Liar." He squeezed her sides lightly, and pulled her impossibly closer.

Fabienne swallowed hard and forced herself into a sitting position despite the protest of her battered body. As her vision steadied, she noticed the care with which Emmanuel had tended to her, as best as he was able. And he was right, she'd had enough energy left for her body to begin healing itself, but not enough to be whole.

It wasn't lost on Fabienne what Emmanuel had done for her. He'd fought and killed. Beyond that, he'd been relentless in doing whatever it took to protect her.

The realization hit her like a sack of bricks in her chest, unexpected and disarming.

A warmth crept up her neck, unbidden. This wasn't the time for distractions. Not when they were still in enemy territory. Not when they were still being hunted. But for once, she threw her caution to the wind. She couldn't stop thinking about everything, all at once. About *him.* He could've left her here and taken off. But he didn't. He chose to fight, and bleed for her instead. The thought of it overwhelmed her. She turned again, blinking up at him.

"What are our odds?"

Emmanuel didn't answer immediately. He leaned forward, pressing his chest to her back, hugging her from behind. He took a deep, steadying breath. His presence was unnervingly steady, and for a moment, she forgot the dangers pressing in around them.

"Well. For starters, the catacombs don't go any further," he said. "This is a dead end."

Rot. "Then, we can't stay here long," she said.

"Not at all."

"We should start making our way out of here."

He tilted his head slightly, his arms holding her tighter. The feeling of safety she felt, here in his arms, made all six of her hearts leap.

"No. Your body needs to heal more. I won't have you moving around just yet—"

The chamber wall exploded. A shockwave tore through the air as stone and debris hurtled toward them. Fabienne didn't think. Bodily agony be damned. In a breath, her wings were out, she'd leapt from Emmanuel's lap, and *moved.* A monstrous, shadowed figure burst through the rubble, its form wreathed in darkness.

The Faedes had found them. And they weren't alone.

Figures poured through the opening—the Fraetèn and the Taétàn.

Emmanuel was already moving. He lunged forward, his blade slicing through the first Fraetèn before the angel could react. Golden blood sprayed across the chamber floor. Another mobster fell before the body of the first even hit the ground.

Fabienne willed her ethèr to life, power flooding through her aching limbs as she met the charge of an oncoming Faede. The creature's jagged, lengthy claws slashed past her face as she ducked, retaliating with a strike of her own.

Her blade met skeletal flesh. The Faede shrieked.

A Taétàn was upon her before she could recover. She twisted, dodging the strike meant to cleave her in two. She fought with every ounce of strength left in her battered body, but she was weakening. Too many were coming too fast.

A cry tore from her lips as she was slammed against the stone wall. The impact stole her breath. A Fraetèn raced for her, his dagger raised—

Then his head snapped back, a blade embedded in his skull.

Fabienne twisted, and found him. Emmanuel. He was a whirlwind of destruction, cutting down their enemies with ruthless precision. Fabienne's vision blurred. She could barely stand. The weight of the battle was crushing them. But Emmanuel was a force of strength, power, and protection. Each time a Fraetèn, Taétàn, or Faede lunged for her, he was there, parrying every move, and blocking them from her.

Fabienne was too weak to defend herself any longer. Her body refused to work. Her wings were weak, she'd lost too much blood, and she wasn't healing fast enough. She wanted desperately to help, to fight back, but she had nothing left to give.

All she could do was trust that Emmanuel would protect her, and get them out of here alive. As she tumbled to the stone, she threw up a final, wordless prayer for Ehyeh to strengthen him. To help him. To give him a way out.

Because Emmanuel Alfonse was now their only hope.

CHAPTER 26

EMMANUEL

The hidden chamber was a storm of blood and steel. Emmanuel's breath came in ragged bursts as he parried a deadly strike from a Fraetèn. The force of the blow almost sent him to his knees. He twisted, using the momentum to drive his own blade through the mobsters neck. The Fraetèn let out a guttural roar before collapsing. There was no time to celebrate the kill. Another came. Then another.

"I do remember saying be entertaining. That didn't mean waste my time," called a familiar voice.

Emmanuel and Fabienne froze.

Noirmother Alexandria Nafariel had come. And another throng of Fraetèn floated behind her.

Burning stars. How would they survive this?

Emmanuel made eye contact with the Noirmother once. Bottomless fury raged in her eyes. She knew he had Désakré, and she'd come to take it.

"Kill them," she said, without emotion. "The star is mine."

Like a coordinated army, the Fraetèn attacked with the full weight of their might.

Fabienne fought at his side, her movements fierce and precise, but she was moving slow. Her breaths were labored. She was a force to be dealt with, but her newfound energy was quickly dissipating. She was exhausted, her wound still stitching itself together. She was weakening. Slowing. Breaking. But still, his pretty little thief kept fighting.

Emmanuel's six hearts burned with a mix of anguish, at her broken body, and immense pride, at her sheer determination to fight, even if it meant to her death. She fought with a practiced grace, weaving through their enemies, her strikes lethal. Blood coated the sleeves of her silver tunic, staining them gold.

Then she'd been bested, wrenched from her feet, and slammed into the stone wall, *hard*. A Fraetèn charged her, but Emmanuel cut him down. The Noirmother floated over and hovered over her body, gloating. The guttural cry that tore from her lips broke something inside of him. Emmanuel roared, draining his Pandemir ethèr. His strength enhanced to that of a behemoth. Every blow he reigned down was fatal.

He killed, again and again, without restraint. Without mercy.

He spun, attacking the Noirmother head on. She met his blows without breaking a sweat, her own ethèr withstanding the barrage of his wrath. He was a storm, but somehow she remained its calm, never faltering or giving up ground. Still, he managed to get the upper hand, swiping out with his wings, slamming their full force into her chest. He shoved the Noirmother back, forcing her away from Fabienne.

Fabienne had given her all, and had paid dearly for it. She laid on the stone, unmoving. Only the slow lift of her chest, and her quiet whimpers, told him she still lived. His vision was stained with darkness as he bulldozed through the swarm of Fraetèn and Taétàn. He had to end this, now.

Emmanuel placed himself between the Noirmother, the oncoming hoard, and Fabienne. He'd die before he let any of them get to her. For every enemy he struck down, two more took their place. The Faedes moved in now, with terrifying speed, their jagged wings slicing through the air, their majik pulsing darkly. Emmanuel barely dodged a series of daggers, shot at his head and throat, one after the other, meant to impale him. He was losing ground. Fast. His strength was running out, and he was running out of weapons.

Then a tremor cracked through the catacombs. Everyone froze. Even the Noirmother turned her head. Clearly this wasn't a part of her plan.

Emmanuel whipped his head around, miffed. "What in the stars..."

The chamber rumbled violently, the walls shaking as if the very foundation of the catacombs had been disturbed. Quick on his feet, Emmanuel spun around, scooped Fabienne up from the floor, and pulled her tight to his chest as he spread his wings and shot into the air.

And not a moment too soon.

The second he was airborne, the ground beneath him groaned and split wide open.

The Fraetèn closest to the rupture let out cries of alarm as the floor gave way beneath them. The chasm spread open like a yawn, swallowing the Fraetèn whole. Their screams faded as their bodies tumbled into everlasting darkness below. Emmanuel was in a state of shock, watching it all. The ground continued to open wide. But while he was able to fly into the air, and balance away from it, the chasm seemed to pull only on the Fraetèn, and it dragged them in. Emmanuel scanned below him, and to his great relief, the Noirmother wasn't exempt. She'd spread her wings, cursing belligerently. She wrestled and fought, trying to fly away.

She couldn't.

The Fraetèn, and their cruel boss, were headed straight for the Hèls.

The Taétàn took one look and scattered. The giants ran off at an incredible speed, easily navigating the dark catacombs, racing away to safety. Even the Faedes pulled away, their faces contorted in horror. The remaining Fraetèn scrambled to retreat, but the chasm was merciless. More cracks spread like veins through the stone, and another section caved in, taking every last one of them, including the beast of a Noirmother, into the abyss. Then just as quickly, the chasm shut itself.

The following silence weighed heavier than any cacophony of sound Emmanuel had ever heard. He floated frozen, his arms gripping Fabienne hard, clutching her tightly to himself. His mind was reeling. What in the burning stars had just happened?

The Faedes, still airborne, recovered quicker.

As one, they shrieked. The sound was piercing, and wholly frightening. Emmanuel felt as if he was trying to fly underwater, as he slowly turned to find the Faedes lunging, all at once.

You will die, Vagabond. Your debt will be paid. Your blood belongs to us, they hissed, as they reached out with their claws. Emmanuel had nowhere else to go. To hide.

And with Fabienne in his arms, there wasn't much else he could do.

"Holy stars," he breathed, at a completely loss. The lifetime of nightmares that followed him everywhere he went, his greatest fears, had all come alive, and were now right in front of him. And there was nothing he could do. "Stars." His eyes burned, hot tears rising. He hadn't cried since he was a youngling. But now, with Fabienne in his arms, and with no way to protect her, to defend her from this, he was terrified that he would, in fact, lose her. Worst of all, he'd lose her at the hands of the Fallen who had taken *everything* from him. The tears fell, and his body began to tremble as the Faedes closed in. "Ehyeh, please. Please! *Rot.* I don't even know how to ask. Help, *please.*"

The Faedes lunged. Emmanuel closed his eyes. He squeezed Fabienne.

"Time," he whispered. "We needed more time." His voice choked as he dropped his face to her hair. "If I ever deserved to have a reason in all the realms, my pretty little thief, to live, love, fight—to be a better aèn—it would be you. Always, forever, it would be you."

Emmanuel took one last breath, and waited for the attack that would kill them both, sending them into the Ellelights—if their fôrs' weren't siphoned and permanently crushed, sending them into a final death as angels.

But it never came.

Instead, the Faedes began to shriek loud, the unnatural sound jarring to his ears. Emmanuel opened his eyes. Fabienne shifted in his arms, turning her head to see what the commotion was. He could see how much the effort cost her. His hearts squeezed.

A light—bright and terrible—had shot down from above and began piercing the Faedes through. The light spread through their figures like veins and burned with liquid fire. Their wings twitched violently, their mouths opening in a soundless scream. Light erupted from within them, consuming them from the inside out.

And as quickly as their torment began, it all ended. The Faedes that hunted him for a lifetime, were dead.

Tears streamed down Emmanuel's cheeks as the weight of it all hit him. His body jerked, and his knees buckled. He tumbled to the stone floor, falling to his knees, carefully releasing Fabienne, all his strength gone.

Emmanuel and Fabienne kneeled in the middle of the carnage, breathless, drenched in blood, and surrounded by the dead. But at last, finally, they were free.

Silence pressed against the chamber, split open to the rest of the catacombs, like a thick shroud. Emmanuel was motionless, unable to process what in the stars had happened.

All of this was impossible. None of it made sense. He was flabbergasted. Absolutely and utterly dumbfounded.

And then, from beside him, between tears and labored breaths, Fabienne tossed back her head, and started laughing.

CHAPTER 27
EMMANUEL

Emmanuel stared wide-eyed at Fabienne, as if she was some gloriously, curious creature from another realm.

Fabienne was bloodied, bruised, and beaten. Yet here she kneeled, snort-cackling so hard tears began rolling down her cheeks. The sound was full, genuine, and unrestrained, echoing through the chamber, and bleeding out into the catacombs. Her laughter was melodious to his ears. A symphony he wanted to enjoy for a lifetime.

Emmanuel blinked down at Fabienne, tears stinging his eyes. This time, they weren't from the fear of losing her. Instead, he was overwhelmed at the great gift he'd been given. The gift of keeping her.

"You're absolutely mad, Fabienne."

And I wholeheartedly adore you for it, he didn't say.

Fabienne hiccuped between peals of laughter. “Me? *You're* the one who prayed to Ehyeh and triggered an apocalypse!”

Emmanuel's lips and ears twitched. “How did you—”

She looked at him, taking in the bewilderment in his eyes. "Oh, you thought I didn't hear?" That only made her laugh harder. "I'm hurting in my body, Emmanuel. Not dead. Of course I heard! And well—"

She gestured to the caved in chamber, now opened to the rest of the catacombs. She wiped at her eyes, grinning wide. “Seems to me you should've used that yap of yours to pray a long time ago. Could've spared us even half of this mess.”

That startled a laugh from him. He tossed his head back, cackling and shaking his head.

“Fabienne Evruel, I swear—”

He didn't finish his words. He threw the weight of himself at her, scooping her up into his arms, burying his face into her hair.

For the first time in what felt like an eternity, Emmanuel let himself breathe. Let himself relax. Let himself explode with all the emotions warring inside of him. He laughed, and he cried. He held onto her, his only lifeline to sanity, to this world. He sobbed, both in gratitude, and in reverence, at their sheer luck.

No, not luck.

Forgiveness. Grace. Unmitigated blessing and mercy.

He sobbed for the lifetime of brokenness and pain, of loss and instability, of hurt and betrayal, all brought to an end, so suddenly, so *easily*, all because of a prayer. All because of *her*. Because of this angel, who simply refused to give up, and somehow, along the way, he'd found it in himself to not give up, either. To try, just one last time.

And it worked. Burning stars, it had *worked.*

They were alive. They were together. They'd survived.

After a long moment, he lifted his head to Fabienne, his hearts pounding. *Rot.* He'd nearly lost her. He'd nearly lost himself. But here she was, broken but beautiful. Scarred, but so rotting perfect. And in the palms of her hands balanced all six of his hearts. Every last one. And he'd be burned to the Hèls if he ever took them back.

Emmanuel wrapped his arms around Fabienne's slender frame, gripping her with a ferocity that would break most of the aèls he'd dealt with in the past. But not her. Never her. Fabienne was strong and unyielding. And he wanted nothing more, nothing else, than for her to be entirely his. He clung to her as if starved for air to breathe. He was desperate to have her, to be with her, in every way, for all of time.

To his surprise, to his great, profound pleasure, Fabienne didn't resist. She melted into his embrace, tucking herself perfectly into him, her curves lined up with his. She folded into his chest, breathing him in. Her nails dug into his leathers, gripping him close. She didn't care about the blood, the dirt, the sweat. He drank her in, and she did the same.

Emmanuel leaned down, his body beginning to shake. When he spoke, his voice was only breath, husky, low, and strained. "I'm sorry. The job at the Armands. The hèls of getting kidnapped by the Noir-mother. This rotting quest. Taking the star... Fabienne. *Rot.* I'm so burning sorry."

Fabienne chuckled, smiling up at him, brushing one of his locs away from his eyes. "I know."

Emmanuel hung his head lower, his eyes glued to her lips. A gnawing hunger, deep inside of him, begged, demanded he claimed her mouth. But he didn't want to force something she wouldn't want. He wrestled with himself, looking from that tempting mouth of hers, then to her eyes.

Fabienne's smile grew wider. Then, she lifted her head, and crushed her mouth against his. Her kiss was devouring. Her body arched into his, demanding more. Emmanuel fell for her, fell with her, and lost himself in the thrill. In that moment, he was completely undone.

The kiss stole the very breath from his lungs. He forgot where they were. Forgot what they'd just survived. Forgot the aches in his body, and the death all around them. Now, in this moment, all that mattered, was Fabienne.

He kissed her, exploring her mouth in ways he'd wanted to do in a private chamber with angel-wine after a hot meal. Not here in these rotting catacombs. But he didn't care. His breath mingled with hers, as she wound her hands through his hair. Her lips were warm and steady, and deliciously curious as she nibbled and tugged, pulling at him.

Emmanuel hadn't known peace for a long time. Now he knew what it looked like. Felt like.

Tasted like.

It was her, and this Great King she hadn't given up on. A Great King who, he learned, had also not given up on him.

He hadn't known what it would take for his world to come together again. He wasn't sure how to create normalcy, or pursue a life, but now, for the first time, he had a shot to figure it out. And he wouldn't have to do it alone.

When they finally pulled apart, they were breathless. Fabienne's breath was tangled with his own, while her arms and legs had wound tight around his wide frame, pressing their bodies together. Her forehead rested against his, gentle and warm.

"My Emmanuel. Thank you for staying with me. Bleeding for me. Stars. I'll never be able to thank Ehyeh enough. You're still here," she choked, fresh tears sliding down her cheeks, her eyes brimming with gratitude and hope.

Emmanuel's throat tightened. "I don't deserve to be."

Her fingers brushed lightly along his jaw, her touch gentle but firm. "You're wrong."

Those two words unraveled him. He'd spent so long believing otherwise. Believing that survival was his punishment. That living was something he had to endure, not something he was allowed to look forward to.

"Emmanuel." Fabienne whispered his name like a prayer. It was all he could do not to fold her, and claim her, all of her, in these stars-forsaken catacombs. Her eyes never wavered from his as she spoke. "You don't have to run anymore."

His nostrils flared. His eyes burned, as a wave of emotion flooded through him violently. He tried to breathe. He failed. The rise of everything he'd ever wanted, but never believed he could have, all began to eclipse him in this moment, threatening to pull him apart.

"I'm here, with you. I swear it."

Emmanuel's jaw quivered, the tears threatening to fall. "For how long?"

"As long as you'll have me," Fabienne whispered. "I would choose you, my Emmanuel. I would have you. All of you. Your mess, your mistakes, your brashness. I would have your pain and your glory. Your recklessness and your cunning. I would have you, for all of my lifetimes. Besides, Tatiana has always wanted a basari."

Emmanuel couldn't take it. The tears fell, freely, overwhelming him. "My precious, Fabienne…"

"Don't push me away," she breathed softly, her lips brushing lightly against his. "Not after everything. Promise me."

Emmanuel's walls cracked. He couldn't stop them. Couldn't stop her. And he didn't want to.

Fabienne broke through his defenses, and he burning well let her.

"I won't go anywhere, Emmanuel." Fabienne's voice was a whisper against his skin, her breath warm and steady. She held his gaze. She knew Emmanuel needed her to see him, the real him, and commit. And she did. "But I need you to stop running."

Running. It was all he'd ever done. But maybe… Maybe he didn't have to anymore.

Emmanuel swallowed, holding Fabienne's gaze, her flame and passion matching his own.

"Fabienne Evruel, by my wings and my fôrs, I swear to you on every lifetime I will live," he breathed, the sacred oath bursting from him fueled by holy fire. "I will not run, from you, from this world, not even from myself, ever again. I am yours, to have and to hold, to cherish and to love. Until we are called to enter the Ellelights."

Fabienne's answering smile was blinding, brighter than the sôlsunes. Brighter than all the stars of the atèmos. She claimed his mouth again, bringing him to an edge he never thought he'd near. When Fabienne pulled Emmanuel off that edge, he let her, as she claimed his hearts, and every single wretched, glorious part of his soul.

CHAPTER 28

FABIENNE

Fabienne Evruel's hearts pounded in her chest like drums, swelling with newfound love, hope, and the miraculous thrall of joy.

Fabienne Evruel, by my wings and my fōrs, I swear to you on every lifetime I will live. I will not run, from you, from this world, not even from myself, ever again. I am yours, to have and to hold, to cherish and to love. Until we are called to enter the Ellelights.

She held Emmanuel tightly, burying her face against his shoulder, repeating his vow to herself, over and over. None of this felt real, but she knew it was all true. Her hearts were full of emotion, elation, and expectation for what was to come.

Emmanuel's arms wrapped around her, his fingers brushing against her back in a silent, reassuring gesture. For a long, uninterrupted moment, they just stayed there, tangled in relief, exhaustion, and something neither of them could quite name, or even say, but they both felt at the very core of their fôrs.

Then, Fabienne remembered.

Désakré.

She pulled back slightly, searching his face. “Where's the star?”

Emmanuel exhaled, his expression sobering. He jut his chin at his satchel that was still in the hollow of the chamber, resting by hers. It was a miracle the Noirmother hadn't seen it, and snatched it away.

“In there.”

Her brows furrowed. “What do we do with it?”

Emmanuel looked out over the many places where the catacombs had caved in. “I honestly have no idea. I'm terrified of the thing. And the moment anyone learns we have it, they'll hunt us down.”

"What if we traded it for a lot of coin?"

Emmanuel snorted. "You'd never do it. You're too good for such petty dealings."

She chuckled. He was right. She wouldn't just discard the star. Not so carelessly, anyway.

"So it stays with us until we figure out what to do with it?"

Emmanuel looked at her. She could see the lines of exhaustion weighing him down. He was worn out. His face was lined with fresh cuts and bruises. He was healing, but like her, the repair was slow. He needed rest. They both did.

He nodded.

"Okay. I'm sure we can bribe someone in the Crying Veil to help us glamour it. Then we can hide it somewhere, until we figure out what to do with it."

Emmanuel grinned, his usual mischief returning to his eyes. "I know just the angel."

Then, something profound shifted in his expression. Raw, heart-aching emotion lined the planes of his handsome face. He balled his hands into fists, and a gut-wrenching sob tore from his throat.

"Fabienne, they're gone," he cried. "All of them."

Fabienne's eyes widened, not catching on. "Who, Emmanuel?"

"The Faedes."

The words left his mouth as a confession, a prayer, and a well of endless gratitude. Fabienne was lost for a moment. Yes, the Fallen angels had been destroyed by an unnatural, holy power. But why was he throwing such a fit?

Then it hit her like a pile of boulders.

The Faedes were gone.

Which meant for the first time in Emmanuel's existence, he was finally free. His gaze met hers, something almost disbelieving in his expression.

"They're *gone*," he repeated. "I don't owe them

anymore. My blood is no longer a debt. I can start over."

Stars.

Holy, stars.

Fabienne's lips parted. She hadn't even thought about it. He was right. The blood debt that had bound him since birth was gone. Never again would Fallen angels hunt him, and try to kill him.

Emmanuel was free.

Emmanuel let out a breathless laugh, shaking his head. "I never thought I'd live long enough to say that."

Fabienne smiled at him, beaming. Her hearts swelled. "What will you do?"

He exhaled, running a hand through his dirt-streaked locs. "Who the rot cares? As long as I have you, it doesn't burning matter. Anything, anywhere, with you is all I desire. Is all I ask."

Her hearts seized, squeezing at the thought.

"I will say this, I'm done with that life," he said firmly. "The thieving. The running. The lying. After everything we just went through?" He shook his head. "I want no parts. I will have nothing to do with it anymore."

Fabienne's hearts ached. She understood him so well, it almost hurt. She had spent so long surviving—

doing whatever it took to pay back her own debts, even when it led her further into darkness.

And now? All she wanted was out, too. But she still owed the Ukaveli. And only a certain piece of jewelry would buy her freedom.

Fabienne's expression turned somber. Emmanuel was free, but she wasn't. Not yet.

Emmanuel must have seen the shadows in her eyes. He shifted almost immediately, before she could dwell on her thoughts. Shimmying beneath her, he reached in the pocket at his thigh, digging inside.

Fabienne watched, confused, as he pulled something out.

Something small. Pulsing. Ivory.

Fabienne squinted in the darkness at the locket.

Then she started screaming.

"Is that *Zazràs*?"

The locket he'd stolen from her. The locket he'd lost, costing her freedom. The one and only thing that would satisfy the Ukaveli enough to clear her final debt.

Less than three dawns later, Emmanuel was holding it. Again.

Emmanuel grinned at her stunned expression. "Snatched it back from the Noirmother while we were fighting. Angels really do have to pay more attention to their valuables, even in the middle of altercations."

She stared at him, wide-eyed. "You—"

He pressed it into her hand. "Take it."

Fabienne blinked. Then the tears started streaming, unbidden.

He wrapped her fingers around the locket. It was warm, and still thrumming with life. The Fallen's fôrs was still inside. The thought made Fabienne shiver, but she clutched the stone regardless.

"Pay off your debt, my pretty answered prayer. And be free."

My pretty answered prayer.

Fabienne lifted her eyes to Emmanuel's, her vision blurry because of her tears. She laughed and sobbed.

The thought of Tatiana filled her mind, and her racking sobs turned to wailing. Stars. She could finally do it. The healing she'd bargained for to keep Tatiana alive. The bargain that claimed her life in servitude as payment. It would finally be paid.

Fabienne sat frozen, her hands curled tightly around *Zazràs*, her breath coming in shallow gasps as hot tears streaked her face. A fresh sob broke from her lips as she looked up at him, at the angel who had been her enemy, was forced to be her partner, and along the way, had become her world.

She barely managed to whisper, "*Thank you.* Endlessly."

Emmanuel's expression softened. A flash flickered in his eyes. He reached up, brushing away a stray tear with his thumb.

"You don't have to thank me," he said, his voice gruff with emotion. "You deserve to be free."

A fresh wave of emotion crashed over her, and before she could stop herself, she threw her arms around him, holding him tight, burying herself against his warmth.

"I'll probably never let you go," she whispered, her voice trembling.

Emmanuel let out a slow breath, his arms tightening around her. "I wouldn't want it any other way."

The words sent a shiver through her.

"Fabienne, let's start over... together." She stared at him, mouth hanging open. "We've been given a second chance, we might as well burning take it."

Her lips parted, and then, despite everything—the pain, the exhaustion, the sheer weight of the last few dawns—she smiled. A big, unrestrained, joyful smile.

"Yes," she breathed. "Yes, let's start over. Together. I would love that."

Before another word could be spoken, she leaned in and kissed him. It was different this time—not frantic or desperate. It was slow and sure. A kiss of new beginnings.

Emmanuel sighed into it, tilting her deeper into his arms, as if sealing everything they had just decided in that moment. When they finally pulled away, breathless, Fabienne let out a small laugh, pressing her forehead against his.

Emmanuel smirked. "I think it's time we got out of these rotting catacombs." A pause. The bob of his throat. "And go home."

Fabienne beamed like the sôlsunes of Xodom.

"You're right," she said, fighting fresh tears. "It's time to go home."

Emmanuel pushed to his feet, keeping Fabienne in his arms. Floating into the air, he hovered past the strewn bodies of the dead, flying to their satchels. Emmanuel triple checked his to make sure Désakré hadn't magically disappeared. Satisfied the star was still in their possession, Emmanuel gently released Fabienne. She was weak, but she could still float along. Hand in hand, fingers intertwined, Fabienne and Emmanuel began flying out of the Taétàn catacombs.

She'd been forced into this quest as a thief desperately seeking an escape. But maybe, all this time, the purpose was to sway a vagabond who needed a reminder that he deserved to be free, too. And this was the only way he'd believe.

They were battered. They were broken. But they were also alive.

And they had each other.

Fabienne and Emmanuel floated through the catacombs, rising higher and higher, in no rush. They didn't have the strength to do more, so they didn't. Together, they flew toward the catacombs entrance, and when they finally made it out, they headed towards the umbrella of Takari. They needed food, shelter, and somewhere to lie low before flying back to Xodom. The world of giants would be the perfect place. Even if Fabienne wanted to see all of their heads roll.

Everyone knew kings were meant to be robbed. Especially from their graves. But Fabienne was glad to learn, not all graves were homes for the dead. Some were secret portals to love, hope, and a new chance at a crazy, curious, life.

AUTHOR'S NOTE

Hello Elledellien,

I'm grateful for you. Thank you for taking the time to read To Sway A Vagabond. I hope you loved reading it as much as I loved writing it.

If you enjoyed this story, would you mind **taking a moment to write a review on my website and on Amazon**?

A few words on how you felt about the story will help me in more ways than you know. Thank you. See you in the next adventure.

Continue your journey: StephanieBwaBwa.com

Glossary

To Sway A Vagabond Lexicon

TO SWAY A VAGABOND GLOSSARY

Atèmos (AH-TEM-MOS): Space; galactic atmosphere; the expanse in the outer universe surrounding the planets.

Aèl (AH-YELL): The angelic term for woman or female.

Aèn (AH-YEN): The angelic term for man or male.

Basari (BA-SA-RIE): Brother in the native language of Domenent angels.

Bedchamber (BED-CHAMBER): Bedroom. Also interchangeable with differing alcoves within an enlarged bedroom suite.

Bedcloud (BED-CLOUD): An angelic bed made entirely of clouds and ethereal matter.

Chariot (CHAIR-EE-UT): A crude Fraetèn transport vehicle, used to detain and transfer bound angels.

Clipped (CLIPPED): Federal punishment for angels who have broken the law. Delinquent angels have every one of their wing pairs broken at the jointed points as clips of steel and ethèr are snapped into the former points of their wings rendering the angels disabled for eternity.

Cloudchair (CLOUD-CHAIR): A chair. Also interchangeable with a single-seater couch.

Cloudcouch (CLOUD-COUCH): A couch. Also interchangeable with loveseats, L-couches, and chamber sitting.

Cosm (KOH-ZUM): Planet.

Craven Wood (CRAY-VEN WOOD): A cursed and ancient forest nestled between Xodom and Taétàn territory. Home to monsters, illusions, and the dying remnants of magic.

Creed (CUH-REED): The law.

Crescent (CRESS-SENT): A deadly assassin within the Crescent Guild. These elite angels serve the Fraetèn, marked by their cruelty, beauty, and absolute loyalty.

Cycle (PSY-CULL): One year.

Darkerèth (DAR-KEH-RETH): A race of dragons who live in the Dèrneveil cosm and throughout the Caelesti realm.

Dawn (DAWN): One day.

Désakré (DAY-ZA-KRAY): A powerful relic believed to contain divine energy capable of both healing and destruction. Hidden deep within a Taétàn king's grave.

Domenent (DO-MEN-ENT): A mid-high angelic rank. Known for six pairs of membranous wings, multicolored eyes, curved ears, and enhanced ethèr. Both feared and revered across Elledelle.

Dusk (DUSK): Night. Also interchangeable with evening.

Dusknite (DUSK-NITE): A black, veil-like cloak or substance that shields its wearer from detection. Blocks ethèr signatures and masks presence from even the most powerful Watchers.

Elledelle (ELLA-DELLE): The universe in which the Elvriel realm and the Rèvaillèl cosm is located.

Elvriel (ELLE-VRIE-UL): An Elledelle realm (dimension). Filled with planets that higher ranking angels call home.

Ethèr (EY-THAIR): Innate, supernatural, magical powers of Etherien angels.

Etherlock (EY-THAIR-LOCK): A supernatural restraint clamped onto angels to suppress their ethèr and immobilize their wings. Commonly used during imprisonment or execution.

Faede (FAYD): A Domenent angel who has fallen from grace. Their fôrs becomes corrupted, and their wings darken, signaling their transformation into a cursed being.

Fallen (FALL-LEN): Disgraced angels who were once Etheriens but have been stripped of their original order and been made into reprobate Fallen.

Fôrs (FORCE): Angelic life energy and spirit. The spirit of angels is a distinct being that dwells inside of them, embodying their ethèr, able to communicate with the conscious of the host angel while fully submissive to commands given by the angel.

Fraetèn (FRAY-TEN): A higher angelic rank often associated with corruption, power, and lawless rule. They oversee guilds, run syndicates, and answer only to the highest thrones.

Higherank (HIGHER-RANK): The title for angels of a higher rank.

Hôr (OARS): Hour.

Hèl (HELL): One of the innumerable names for "hell" in the Elledelle universe.

Mekàd (MAY-KAD): Month.

Noirfather (NWAHR-FAW-THUR): A ruling title for male Fraetèn lords who control syndicates and corrupted guilds.

Noirmother (NWAHR-MUH-THUR): The female counterpart to a Noirfather. Wields dominion over lesser Fraetèn and Crescents.

Noirlordes (NWAHR-LORDS): Lieutenants under a Noirfather or Noirmother. Lead operations, command hunts, and enforce syndicate rule with violence and authority.

Palàs (PAH-LAHS): An angelic stronghold or estate. Typically protected by Watchers and infused with protective ethèr wards.

Pasaille (PA-SIGH): Paradise. Interchangeable with eternity or a celestial place angels transcend to after death.

Pasari (PA-SA-RIE): Father in the native language of Domnen angels.

Portal Keeper (POR-TUL-KEY-PUR): A mysterious being who guards sacred or forbidden gates between realms. Their power is ancient and rarely understood.

Rotpot (ROT-POT): A derogatory term to call someone an idiot or a piece of rot.

Shaith (SHAYTH): Horrific shadow-trackers summoned by the Fraetèn.

Siphoner (SIGH-FO-NUR): An angel who can extract the fôrs from others, consuming or transferring it through physical contact.

Sisari (SEE-SA-RIE): Sister in the native language of Domenent angels.

Sôlsunes (SOLE-SOONS): Suns.

Taétàn (TAY-AY-TAHN): Towering, titan-like beings from the moon Takari. Known for their haunting beauty, immense power, and brutal glamour.

Takari (TAH-KA-REE): A moon orbiting Elvriel, inhabited by the enigmatic Taétàn. The air is dense with golden mist, and the gravity bends ethèr in unpredictable ways.

Watchers (WAH-CHURZ): Elite angelic warriors tasked with guarding Palàs estates, celestial gates, and sacred places. Highly trained and utterly loyal.

Wèk (WEH-K): One week.

Winglock (WING-LOCK): A restraint used to seal an angel's wings, preventing flight and access to ethèr.

Xodom (ZAU-DUM): A sprawling megalopolis at the heart of the Rèvaillèl cosm. Cloaked in dusk and ruled by shadows, Xodom is the epicenter of Fraetèn power, black markets, and celestial corruption. Its labyrinthine streets house syndicates, cursed shrines, fallen angels, and relic hunters.

Youngling (YOUNG-LING): Young angel. Interchangeable with adolescent or teenager.

Zazràs (ZAZ-RAHS): A mysterious locket containing the fôrs of a bound Fallen.

THE ADVENTURES CONTINUE

I hope you loved Fabienne and Emmanuel's story as much as I do. If you're hungry for more, the universe continues to expand.

If you're ready to keep reading, visit: **StephanieBwaBwa.com** to find your next adventure. Until next time, see you in Elledelle.

- Stephanie

ELLEDELLE STORIES

In the Beginning

Natalia

Tempting Thieves

To Sway A Vagabond

Of Seas and Tides

Trapped By Pirates

The Ethereal Kings

Barbarian of the Stars

Starry Kingdoms of the Fae

Bound By Watchers

ABOUT THE IMMERSIONEER

Stephanie BwaBwa is a best-selling epic romance fantasy author who writes cinematic, immersive, character-driven stories where troubled souls rise through darkness and corruption to find freedom, healing, hope, and love.

She's the founder of Elledelle Entertainment, a company dedicated to publishing and producing stories in: Elledelle—the fantasy universe of beloved winged creatures, captivating readers worldwide.

Also a Christian and Afro-Caribbean, you can usually find her reading with too many snacks. Wings high!

Get Connected: StephanieBwaBwa.com

www.ingramcontent.com/pod-product-compliance
Lightning Source LLC
Chambersburg PA
CBHW070548310726
48982CB00011B/1497/J
* 9 7 9 8 9 8 7 2 1 2 8 6 8 *